Discoverying Western Short Stories

Oscar Wilde / James Joyce / Kate Chopin / Charlotte Perkins Gilman
Edgar Alan Poe / Jack London / Steven Reeder / Joseph Conrad
Alphonse Daudet / Nathaniel Hawthorne / Dylan Thomas

The Close and Holy Darkness

Ok-sun Kang / Steven Reeder

Shinasa

The Close and Holy Darkness: Discovering Western Short Stories

By
Oksun Kang
Steven Reeder

SHINASA Publishing Co.
28-36 2F Nokbeon-Dong Eunpyung-Ku Seoul, Korea
Registered: 9-52 (January 5, 1956)
Tel: (02) 382-6411
Fax: (02) 382-6401
E-mail: shinasa@chollian.net
Homepage: www.shinasa.co.kr

First published JUNE 30, 2006

Price: 정가 15,000원

ISBN: 89-8396-535-5

Contents

Unheard of Contradictions: A Prologue

Short stories are a dying art form. Few artists write them because fewer people are reading them. The market isn't what it used to be. In fact, movies have all but replaced short stories. Movies, having to be short themselves, are nothing more than short stories on screen. Short stories, like movies, usually follow a single point of view and have time or space to pursue a single major plotline with only a few well fleshed out central characters. Such structure gives the movies accessibility. It also makes short stories a wonderful window to the world that can be glanced upon in just one reading session. Reading short stories allows us to go deeper into the story than a novel and to savor the techniques the writer uses to draw a picture in our mind. Short stories are like movies, except we control the visuals. How sad it is losing popularity.

The very artistic nature of short stories also makes them more difficult to read. The language is often more poetic and the choice of words more deliberate. This can make it difficult for a student whose second language is English. An exercise in literary appreciation can turn into frustration. Enter *Discovering Western Short Stories*. The purpose of this book is rather simple: to introduce second language learners to the wonderful prose of short stories. To make them more accessible, we have introduced the authors with a brief biography that can help students understand the environment and situations in which they were written. A simple synopsis is also included to help the student understand the story before it is read so as to help focus more on the language rather than on trying to understand the basic plot. Since all of these stories were written more than sixty years ago, many words and expressions are either archaic or have changed in meaning. To make it easier for the student to know the exact meaning of difficult words or idioms, a simple explanation is offered at the end of each story. And finally, to facilitate a greater and deeper meaning from the stories, study questions are offered to encourage a second or third look at the text and even to base essays on. A glossary of literary terms can be found in the appendix to introduce students to the various techniques of reading, writing, and studying short fiction.

The choice of authors was rather simple. We chose writers whose works were offered on the public domain; this means their copyrights have not been renewed and have expired sixty years after their death, with the exception of "Für Elise," which was written six years ago, and we were given permission to print it. We tried to choose a good balance of British and American authors, and we even chose a Canadian and French one too. We also wanted to have a balance of different literary genres: fairy tales by Oscar Wilde and James Joyce; feminist stories by Kate Chopin and Charlotte Perkins Gilman; horror by Edgar Alan Poe; patriotic by Alphonse Daudet; a Christmas tale by Dylan Thomas; literary fiction by Joseph Conrad and Jack London; and even an experimental story by one of the editors. In other words, our collection of short stories is somewhat like the curious yellow wallpaper in

Charlotte Perkins Gilman's same named story whose patterns confuse through "unheard of contradictions." These stories may seem like "unheard of contradictions" that confuse and irritate; some may even seem as pointless as the outrageous patterns on the wallpaper, yet we have tried our best to make these stories as accessible as possible.

And finally, the rather original title to this collection □ The Close and Holy Darkness □ is a line from Dylan Thomas' "A Child's Christmas in Wales." The feelings these words conjure in the mind actually are far from oxymoronic. In fact, they describe rather well the feelings the come when we just sit back, read, and let the story overcome our emotions. The tales actually envelope us like "the close and holy darkness," allowing us to feel quite at home in these foreign accounts of far away people and places.

It is our hope that students will find these selections as enjoyable as we do. Nothing of great worth is ever obtained easily and getting to know these stories intimately is no exception. But with effort and patience, these stories will stay within our memories for the rest of our lives.

Steven Reeder
Dongseo University

I. THE HAPPY PRINCE

by Oscar Wilde

Author

Synopsis

Text

Words & Idioms

Study Questions

INTRODUCTION OF THE AUTHOR:

Oscar Wilde (1854-1900)

Though Oscar Wilde lived his later life in controversy and even suffered arrest, he has since been redeemed as an original poet, one of the greatest playwrights of the Victorian Age, and an influence on the youth through his fairy tales. Oscar was born on October 16, 1854 to a philanthropist father, Sir William Wilde, who opened his medical clinic for ear and eye disease to the poor and needy, and an educated mother, Francesca Wilde, who as a journalist and a poet wrote her poetry under the pseudonym, "Speranza." Oscar was home schooled as a child and later went on to graduate from Trinity College, Dublin. While in college his prowess with words surfaced and he won various awards and scholarships for his works, especially poetry. He fell in love with Florence Balcome who later got engaged to Bram Stoker, of later *Dracula* fame. The loss of his love was one of the causes for Wilde to leave Ireland and start on a successful career as a traveling lecturer in America, London, and Paris from 1881 to 1882.

In 1884, he married Constance Lloyd, an educated woman, and had two children in succession the following two years. Perhaps forced to make a living for his family, Wilde's greatest efforts followed for the next six years. In 1888, he published a collection of children's fairy tales *The Happy Prince and Other Tales*. His only novel, *The Picture of Dorian Gray* (1891), was published a year earlier in short story form for an American magazine and was met with critical disappointment, though it is considered a classic now. He followed this with a second collection of children's stories, *The House of Pomegranates* (1892). Though he did publish collections of poetry, Wilde is most famous as a dramatist, his most popular being the very witty *The Importance of Being Earnest* (1895).

Yet out of all his success, Wilde's carefree lifestyle in the Victorian Age was his downfall. First hinted at when he wrote of Shakespeare's famous sonnets being addressed to a boy, Wilde's own sexuality became a scandal as well. Wilde began to have a sexual relationship with a young fan, a seventeen year old boy at the time, which set the boy's father off in a rage. The father publicly slandered Wilde, whereupon Wilde sued. The truth of Wilde's homosexuality was eventually brought out in the trial, and Wilde was arrested for it (a crime at the time called "gross indecency"). He was subjected to two years of hard labor, which ruined his health. Upon his release, he changed his name and lived a life of poverty, when, three years later, he died of cerebral meningitis in Paris on November 30, 1900. Wilde may have died in shame, but his work and genius live on as adults and children alike read and respect his works as true classics.

Synopsis

In a city long ago stood the statue of the Happy Prince that was covered with gold and adorned with precious jewels. The statue of the prince looked happy, but many in the city were not; they looked just like the Happy Prince felt inside, destitute. Like all cities, the rich went about their business indifferent to the plight of the poor. The statue used to be human and never cared for the poor until his death sent his soul into the statue. The statue of the Happy Prince was an inspiration to all; even the animal kingdom felt inspired by its beauty.

A rather foolish swallow that fell in love with beautiful things in nature became distracted by the statue's beauty and fell in love with it. It made a nest and lived with the Happy Prince. Yet the prince was not happy; he was sad and cried real tears for the suffering and the poor. His lot in life was to view all the ugliness and misery in and around the city. Though he was clothed in gold with sapphires for eyes, he could not bear to see the people go without their basic needs.

As winter approached, the swallow felt it was time to fly away to Egypt where it was warm. The Happy Prince asked the bird to take the jewel from his sword and give it to those who needed it the most. He then asked the swallow to tear out his sapphire eyes, and when they were put to better use, commanded the swallow to take the gold leafing covering his body and make sure the poor had food and clothing for the winter. Throughout the long, cold winter, the swallow dreamed of the warmth and wonder of Egypt, yet it helped the statue do good deeds though it cost the bird its life. The little swallow realized that the worth of life is greater than its own. And though the Happy Prince was now blind, the bird would stay the rest of the winter to fly over the city to be the Prince's eyes and messenger of charity. Yet the cold of winter was too much for the swallow and it died.

The Happy Prince was eventually torn down due to its ugliness and melted in a fire to be reused. Yet its leaden heart would not melt and was thrown out, only to be rescued by two angels sent by God who were ordered to find the two most precious things in the city: they brought the dead bird and the leaden heart. They had chosen wisely.

TEXT

High above the city, on a tall column, stood the statue of the Happy Prince. He was gilded all over with thin leaves of fine gold, for eyes he had two bright sapphires, and a large red ruby glowed on his sword-hilt.

He was very much admired indeed. 'He is as beautiful as a weathercock,' remarked one of the Town Councillors who wished to gain a reputation for having artistic tastes; 'only not quite so useful,' he added, fearing lest people should think him unpractical, which he really was not.

'Why can't you be like the Happy Prince?' asked a sensible mother of her little boy who was crying for the moon. 'The Happy Prince never dreams of crying for anything.'

'I am glad there is some one in the world who is quite happy,' muttered a disappointed man as he gazed at the wonderful statue.

'He looks just like an angel,' said the Charity Children as they came out of the cathedral in their bright scarlet cloaks, and their clean white pinafores.

'How do you know?' said the Mathematical Master, 'you have never seen one.'

'Ah! but we have, in our dreams,' answered the children; and the Mathematical Master frowned and looked very severe, for he did not approve of children dreaming.

One night there flew over the city a little Swallow. His

friends had gone away to Egypt six weeks before, but he had stayed behind, for he was in love with the most beautiful Reed. He had met her early in the spring as he was flying down the river after a big yellow moth, and had been so attracted by her slender waist that he had stopped to talk to her.

'Shall I love you?' said the Swallow, who liked to come to the point at once, and the Reed made him a low bow. So he flew round and round her, touching the water with his wings, and making silver ripples. This was his courtship, and it lasted all through the summer.

'It is a ridiculous attachment,' twittered the other Swallows, 'she has no money, and far too many relations;' and indeed the river was quite full of Reeds. Then, when the autumn came, they all flew away.

After they had gone he felt lonely, and began to tire of his lady-love. 'She has no conversation,' he said, 'and I am afraid that she is a coquette, for she is always flirting with the wind.' And certainly, whenever the wind blew, the Reed made the most graceful curtsies. 'I admit that she is domestic,' he continued, 'but I love travelling, and my wife, consequently, should love travelling also.'

'Will you come away with me?' he said finally to her; but the Reed shook her head, she was so attached to her home.

'You have been trifling with me,' he cried, 'I am off to the Pyramids. Good-bye!' and he flew away.

All day long he flew, and at night-time he arrived at the city. 'Where shall I put up?' he said; 'I hope the town has made preparations.'

Then he saw the statue on the tall column. 'I will put up there,' he cried; 'it is a fine position with plenty of fresh air.' So he alighted just between the feet of the Happy Prince.

'I have a golden bedroom,' he said softly to himself as he looked round, and he prepared to go to sleep; but just as he was putting his head under his wing a large drop of water fell on him. 'What a curious thing!' he cried, 'there is not a single cloud in the sky, the stars are quite clear and bright, and yet it is raining. The climate in the north of Europe is really dreadful. The Reed used to like the rain, but that was merely her selfishness.'

Then another drop fell.

'What is the use of a statue if it cannot keep the rain off?' he said; 'I must look for a good chimney-pot,' and he determined to fly away.

But before he had opened his wings, a third drop fell, and he looked up, and saw □ Ah! what did he see?

The eyes of the Happy Prince were filled with tears, and tears were running down his golden cheeks. His face was so beautiful in the moonlight that the little Swallow was filled with pity.

'Who are you?' he said.

'I am the Happy Prince.'

'Why are you weeping then?' asked the Swallow; 'you have quite drenched me.'

'When I was alive and had a human heart,' answered the statue, 'I did not know what tears were, for I lived in the palace of Sans-Souci, where sorrow is not allowed to enter. In the daytime I played with my companions in the garden, and in the evening I led the dance in the Great Hall. Round the garden ran a very lofty wall, but I never cared to ask what lay beyond it, everything about me was so beautiful. My courtiers called me the Happy Prince, and happy indeed I was, if pleasure be happiness. So I lived, and so I died. And now that I am dead they have set me up here so high that I can see all the ugliness and all the misery of my city, and though my heart is made of lead yet I cannot choose but weep.'

'What, is he not solid gold?' said the Swallow to himself. He was too polite to make any personal remarks out loud.

'Far away,' continued the statue in a low musical voice, 'far away in a little street there is a poor house. One of the windows is open, and through it I can see a woman seated at a table. Her face is thin and worn, and she has coarse, red hands, all pricked by the needle, for she is a seamstress. She is embroidering passion-flowers on a satin gown for the loveliest of the Queen's maids-of-honour to wear at the next Court-ball. In a bed in the corner of the room her little boy is lying ill. He has a fever, and is asking for oranges. His mother has nothing to give him but river water, so he is crying. Swallow, Swallow, little Swallow, will you not bring her the ruby out of my sword-hilt? My feet are fastened to this pedestal and I cannot move.'

'I am waited for in Egypt,' said the Swallow. 'My friends are flying up and down the Nile, and talking to the large lotus-flowers. Soon they will go to sleep in the tomb of the great King. The King is there himself in his painted coffin. He is wrapped in yellow linen, and embalmed with spices.

Round his neck is a chain of pale green jade, and his hands are like withered leaves.'

'Swallow, Swallow, little Swallow,' said the Prince, 'will you not stay with me for one night, and be my messenger? The boy is so thirsty, and the mother so sad.'

'I don't think I like boys,' answered the Swallow. 'Last summer, when I was staying on the river, there were two rude boys, the miller's sons, who were always throwing stones at me. They never hit me, of course; we swallows fly far too well for that, and besides, I come of a family famous for its agility; but still, it was a mark of disrespect.'

But the Happy Prince looked so sad that the little Swallow was sorry. 'It is very cold here,' he said; 'but I will stay with you for one night, and be your messenger.'

'Thank you, little Swallow,' said the Prince.

So the Swallow picked out the great ruby from the Prince's sword, and flew away with it in his beak over the roofs of the town.

He passed by the cathedral tower, where the white marble angels were sculptured. He passed by the palace and heard the sound of dancing. A beautiful girl came out on the balcony with her lover. 'How wonderful the stars are,' he said to her, and how wonderful is the power of love!'

'I hope my dress will be ready in time for the State-ball,' she answered; 'I have ordered passion-flowers to be embroidered on it; but the seamstresses are so lazy.'

He passed over the river, and saw the lanterns hanging

to the masts of the ships. He passed over the Ghetto, and saw the old Jews bargaining with each other, and weighing out money in copper scales. At last he came to the poor house and looked in. The boy was tossing feverishly on his bed, and the mother had fallen asleep, she was so tired. In he hopped, and laid the great ruby on the table beside the woman's thimble. Then he flew gently round the bed, fanning the boy's forehead with his wings. 'How cool I feel,' said the boy, 'I must be getting better;' and he sank into a delicious slumber.

Then the Swallow flew back to the Happy Prince, and told him what he had done. 'It is curious,' he remarked, 'but I feel quite warm now, although it is so cold.'

'That is because you have done a good action,' said the Prince. And the little Swallow began to think, and then he fell asleep. Thinking always made him sleepy.

When day broke he flew down to the river and had a bath. 'What a remarkable phenomenon,' said the Professor of Ornithology as he was passing over the bridge. 'A swallow in winter!' And he wrote a long letter about it to the local newspaper. Every one quoted it, it was full of so many words that they could not understand.

'To-night I go to Egypt,' said the Swallow, and he was in high spirits at the prospect. He visited all the public monuments, and sat a long time on top of the church steeple. Wherever he went the Sparrows chirruped, and said to each other, 'What a distinguished stranger!' so he enjoyed himself very much.

When the moon rose he flew back to the Happy Prince.

'Have you any commissions for Egypt?' he cried; 'I am just starting.'

'Swallow, Swallow, little Swallow,' said the Prince, 'will you not stay with me one night longer?'

'I am waited for in Egypt,' answered the Swallow. 'To-morrow my friends will fly up to the Second Cataract. The river-horse couches there among the bulrushes, and on a great granite throne sits the God Memnon. All night long he watches the stars, and when the morning star shines he utters one cry of joy, and then he is silent. At noon the yellow lions come down to the water's edge to drink. They have eyes like green beryls, and their roar is louder than the roar of the cataract.'

'Swallow, Swallow, little Swallow,' said the prince, 'far away across the city I see a young man in a garret. He is leaning over a desk covered with papers, and in a tumbler by his side there is a bunch of withered violets. His hair is brown and crisp, and his lips are red as a pomegranate, and he has large and dreamy eyes. He is trying to finish a play for the Director of the Theatre, but he is too cold to write any more. There is no fire in the grate, and hunger has made him faint.'

'I will wait with you one night longer,' said the Swallow, who really had a good heart. 'Shall I take him another ruby?'

'Alas! I have no ruby now,' said the Prince; 'my eyes are all that I have left. They are made of rare sapphires, which were brought out of India a thousand years ago. Pluck out one of them and take it to him. He will sell it to the jeweller, and buy food and firewood, and finish his play.'

'Dear Prince,' said the Swallow, 'I cannot do that;' and he began to weep.

'Swallow, Swallow, little Swallow,' said the Prince, 'do as I command you.'

So the Swallow plucked out the Prince's eye, and flew away to the student's garret. It was easy enough to get in, as there was a hole in the roof. Through this he darted, and came into the room. The young man had his head buried in his hands, so he did not hear the flutter of the bird's wings, and when he looked up he found the beautiful sapphire lying on the withered violets.

'I am beginning to be appreciated,' he cried; 'this is from some great admirer. Now I can finish my play,' and he looked quite happy.

The next day the Swallow flew down to the harbour. He sat on the mast of a large vessel and watched the sailors hauling big chests out of the hold with ropes. 'Heave a-hoy!' they shouted as each chest came up. 'I am going to Egypt!' cried the Swallow, but nobody minded, and when the moon rose he flew back to the Happy Prince.

'I am come to bid you good-bye,' he cried.

'Swallow, Swallow, little Swallow,' said the Prince, 'will you not stay with me one night longer?'

'It is winter,' answered the Swallow, 'and the chill snow will soon be here. In Egypt the sun is warm on the green palm-trees, and the crocodiles lie in the mud and look lazily about them. My companions are building a nest in the Temple of Baalbec, and the pink and white doves are watching them, and cooing to each other. Dear Prince, I must leave you, but I will never forget you, and next spring I will bring you back two beautiful jewels in place of those you have given away. The ruby shall be redder than a red rose, and the sapphire shall be as blue as the great sea.'

'In the square below,' said the Happy Prince, 'there stands a little match-girl. She has let her matches fall in the gutter, and they are all spoiled. Her father will beat her if she does not bring home some money, and she is crying. She has no shoes or stockings, and her little head is bare. Pluck out my other eye, and give it to her, and her father will not beat her.'

'I will stay with you one night longer,' said the Swallow, 'but I cannot pluck out your eye. You would be quite blind then.'

'Swallow, Swallow, little Swallow,' said the Prince, 'do as I command you.'

So he plucked out the Prince's other eye, and darted down with it. He swooped past the match-girl, and slipped the jewel into the palm of her hand. 'What a lovely bit of glass,' cried the little girl; and she ran home, laughing.

Then the Swallow came back to the Prince. 'You are blind now,' he said, 'so I will stay with you always.'

'No, little Swallow,' said the poor Prince, 'you must go away to Egypt.'

'I will stay with you always,' said the Swallow, and he slept at the Prince's feet.

All the next day he sat on the Prince's shoulder, and told him stories of what he had seen in strange lands. He told him of the red ibises, who stand in long rows on the banks of the Nile, and catch gold fish in their beaks; of the Sphinx, who is as old as the world itself and lives in the desert, and knows everything; of the merchants, who walk slowly by the side of their camels, and carry amber beads in their hands; of the King of the Mountains of the Moon, who is as black as ebony, and worships a large crystal; of the great green snake that sleeps in a palm-tree, and has twenty priests to feed it with honey-cakes; and of the pygmies who sail over a big lake on large flat leaves, and are always at war with the butterflies.

'Dear little Swallow,' said the Prince, 'you tell me of marvellous things, but more marvellous than anything is the suffering of men and of women. There is no Mystery so great as Misery. Fly over my city, little Swallow, and tell me what you see there.'

So the Swallow flew over the great city, and saw the rich making merry in their beautiful houses, while the beggars were sitting at the gates. He flew into dark lanes, and saw the white faces of starving children looking out listlessly at the black streets. Under the archway of a bridge two little boys were lying in one another's arms to try and keep themselves warm. 'How hungry we are!' they said. 'You must not lie here,' shouted the Watchman, and they wandered out into the rain.

Then he flew back and told the Prince what he had seen.

'I am covered with fine gold,' said the Prince, 'you must

take it off, leaf by leaf, and give it to my poor; the living always think that gold can make them happy.'

Leaf after leaf of the fine gold the Swallow picked off, till the Happy Prince looked quite dull and grey. Leaf after leaf of the fine gold he brought to the poor, and the children's faces grew rosier, and they laughed and played games in the street. 'We have bread now!' they cried.

Then the snow came, and after the snow came the frost. The streets looked as if they were made of silver, they were so bright and glistening; long icicles like crystal daggers hung down from the eaves of the houses, everybody went about in furs, and the little boys wore scarlet caps and skated on the ice.

The poor little Swallow grew colder and colder, but he would not leave the Prince, he loved him too well. He picked up crumbs outside the baker's door where the baker was not looking, and tried to keep himself warm by flapping his wings.

But at last he knew that he was going to die. He had just strength to fly up to the Prince's shoulder once more. 'Good-bye, dear Prince!' he murmured, 'will you let me kiss your hand?'

'I am glad that you are going to Egypt at last, little Swallow,' said the Prince, 'you have stayed too long here; but you must kiss me on the lips, for I love you.'

'It is not to Egypt that I am going,' said the Swallow. 'I am going to the House of Death. Death is the brother of Sleep, is he not?'

And he kissed the Happy Prince on the lips, and fell

down dead at his feet.

At that moment a curious crack sounded inside the statue, as if something had broken. The fact is that the leaden heart had snapped right in two. It certainly was a dreadfully hard frost. Early the next morning the Mayor was walking in the square below in company with the Town Councillors. As they passed the column he looked up at the statue: 'Dear me! how shabby the Happy Prince looks!' he said.

'How shabby indeed!' cried the Town Councillors, who always agreed with the Mayor, and they went up to look at it.

'The ruby has fallen out of his sword, his eyes are gone, and he is golden no longer,' said the Mayor; 'in fact, he is little better than a beggar!'

'Little better than a beggar' said the Town councillors.

'And here is actually a dead bird at his feet!' continued the Mayor. 'We must really issue a proclamation that birds are not to be allowed to die here.' And the Town Clerk made a note of the suggestion.

So they pulled down the statue of the Happy Prince. 'As he is no longer beautiful he is no longer useful,' said the Art Professor at the University.

Then they melted the statue in a furnace, and the Mayor held a meeting of the Corporation to decide what was to be done with the metal. 'We must have another statue, of course,' he said, 'and it shall be a statue of myself.'

'Of myself,' said each of the Town Councillors, and they quarrelled. When I last heard of them they were quarrelling still.

'What a strange thing!' said the overseer of the workmen at the foundry. 'This broken lead heart will not melt in the furnace. We must throw it away.' So they threw it on a dust-heap where the dead Swallow was also lying.

'Bring me the two most precious things in the city,' said God to one of His Angels; and the Angel brought Him the leaden heart and the dead bird.

'You have rightly chosen,' said God, 'for in my garden of Paradise this little bird shall sing for evermore, and in my city of gold the Happy Prince shall praise me.'

EXPLANATION OF
Words & Idioms

Alas! (interj) an expression used when sad or disappointed.

Baalbec: (n) a Syrian city in Biblical times now destroyed.

Beryl: (n) a precious stone or gem usually the color of white, green, blue, yellow, or pink.

Bulrush: (n) a tall grass-like plant that grows in clusters in marshes, similar to a reed.

Cataract: (n) a large waterfall found on the Nile.

Chimney-pot: (n) a metal pipe added to the top of a chimney.

Chirrup: (v) the chirping sound a bird makes.

Commission: (n) asking to carry out a certain job.

Coo: (v) (the sound a dove or pigeon makes.

Coquette: (n) a flirtatious woman.

Courtiers: (n) people who attend a king's court. Entourage is the modern term.

Curtsey: (n) the type of bow a female makes by bending the knees with one foot forward and holding the dress out to the side with both hands.

Dart: (v) a sudden or fast movement as if throwing a dart.

Distinguished: (adj.) excellent; well-known in a positive way.

Drench: (v) to get completely wet.

Eaves: (n) the part of the roof that hangs over the bottom

edge, usually to catch water.

Ebony: (adj) very dark brown or black.

Embalm: (v) to replace the blood in a dead body with a preservative liquid.

Embroider: (v) to make (clothing, rugs) through needlecraft.

Foundry: (n) a place where metal is melted and worked into various shapes.

Garret: (n) a dismal room located in the top part of a house, similar to an attic.

Ghetto: (n) the old part of a city that is run down and occupied by minority groups.

Gilded: (v) to cover with gold

Glisten: (v) to sparkle in the sunlight.

Grate: (n) an older word for fireplace.

Heave a-hoy: an expression used to tell someone to pull hard on a rope, especially sailors.

Ibis: (n) a type of bird found in Egypt that has a narrow curving beak.

Listlessly: (adv) without energy.

Memnon: (n) a demigod of Persia.

Miller: (n) a worker in a mill (a place that grinds wheat).

Ornithology: (n) related to the study of birds.

Pinafore: (n) a type of sleeveless apron that small girls usually wear over a dress.

Pluck: (v) to remove with the fingers (or, in this case, a beak).

Prospect: (n) the possibility that something planned will happen.

Pygmies: (pl. n) a mythological race of small creatures

similar to fairies, but lacking wings.

Sans-Souci: (n) either a fictional palace or perhaps a palace built (1745-47) at Potsdam, Germany, by Frederick II.

Second Cataract: (n) the second waterfall found on the Nile near Nubia (south Egypt).

Shabby: (adj) old and worn out.

Steeple: (n) the tallest point or tower on a church.

Swallow: (n) a small, swift flying bird usually with a forked tail.

Thimble: (n) a small cup that fits on the finger; it is used while sewing.

Trifle: (v) to not take a subject seriously; a joke or a jest.

Twitter: (v) to laugh at or tease, especially when someone does something embarrassing.

Weathercock: (n) a weather vane in the shape of rooster that showed the direction of the wind and usually sat on top of a barn.

Withered: (adj) to be dried up and shrunken.

Study Questions

1. This is one of the rare works of fiction that is written in fairy tale form. What makes this story read as a fairy tale compared to the other stories?

2. The Grimm fairy tales were often dark and had often ended badly for the protagonists. After the modern fairy tales of Wilde and others were made popular, Grimm's fairy tales were often altered to a more favorable ending. If you compare Wilde's fairy tales, which are considered some of the original fairy tales in English, with the fairy tales made popular by the Brothers Grimm about a half a century earlier, what makes this story different from the earlier ones? Visit http://www.cs.cmu.edu/~spok/grimmtmp/ to review various Gimm Brothers' fairy tales.

3. *The Happy Prince* can also be read as an allegory: an extended metaphor where the characters have meanings outside the actual story. Reread the story. The story tells of a statue and a bird. What is Wilde actually talking about outside the story (this is the allegory of the story)? Who or what do the Mayor and Town Councillors actually represent? The Professor of Ornithology? The Town Clerk? The Art Professor?

4. Why does Wilde have his birds fly away to Egypt? What is the significance of mentioning Egypt and all its wonders in the tale?

5. What is the meaning of having the prince turn into a statue and having a heart of lead that would not melt and then tossed into the trash?

6. What role does the swallow play in this tale? How important is it to have a swallow in the plot? Could it have been another animal? Why or why not? What is the allegorical meaning behind the swallow?

II. Araby

by James Joyce

Author

Synopsis

Text

Words & Idioms

Story Questions

INTRODUCTION OF THE AUTHOR:

James Joyce (1882-1941)

Hailed as one of the greatest writers of the 20th Century, James Joyce was born in Dublin, Ireland on February 2, 1882, the oldest of ten children. He was raised by a father, who was known to waste money, and a devout Catholic mother. By the age of six, he was sent to Belvedere College for a Catholic education under Jesuit priests with the hopes that he would later become a priest. Living in Ireland that sought constant liberation from British rule, Joyce eventually left out of the need to distance himself from what he thought of as a losing battle. Though he lived in poverty as an English teacher in several countries, he wrote everyday and, perhaps out of homesickness, often returned to the city of his birth in his works of fiction with such delicate detail that a reader who has never visited Dublin would intimately know of all its details. He collected his short stories in his first publication, *Dubliners* (1914).

James Joyce is considered the father of stream of consciousness, a literary form where the author strays as far away from the rules of normal writing to the point where the reader is given the sense that he or she is "reading" the mind of the narrator. Punctuation, quotation marks, and other conventional forms of grammar may be removed to add to the effect. Since the mind wanders as it thinks freely, so does the text of the narrator, often creating confusion. *Dubliners*, which includes the short story "Araby," started to exhibit early forms of stream of consciousness, but not until his semi-autobiographical novel *A Portrait of the Artist as a Young Man* (1914) and his literary masterpiece *Ulysses* (1922) did it come to the fore. *Ulysses* also started out as a short story to be featured in *Dubliners*, but the idea of expanding the story to include the daily life of a man as an anti-heroic journey in imitation of Homer's Odyssey turned into a 750 + page book.

Ulysses covered the day in the life, while his next great work of fiction covered the dream ridden haunts of the night in *Finnegan's Wake* (1939). Taking over 17 years to write, it is no wonder Joyce hailed it as the greatest achievement of his profession, having discarded all plot devices and employing stream of consciousness to the maximum. During the writing of this book, Joyce started to go blind, having close friends write what he dictated, much the way the blind Milton would dictate *Paradise Lost*. Joyce also suffered from stomach cramps before its publication. When it was published, the literary world did not know what to make of it. Only with the study and understanding of stream of consciousness did the genius of the work come out.

As World War II swept through Europe, Joyce feared that all he had worked for would be lost as France, where he was living at the time, became occupied by the Nazi's. He was forced to move to Zurich, Switzerland, where his stomach pains continued. On January 13, 1941, after an operation to remove an ulcer, he quietly passed away after saying his goodbyes to his loved ones. He was 51. Joyce may have died in his writing prime, but the legacy he left behind changed the way we would read and write fiction for ever more.

Synopsis

The unnamed narrator of the story relates the memory of his first love and a rather simple quest he set off on to win her affections. His quest starts when he sees the sister of one of his friends standing out on the porch in the quiet street of their neighborhood. The narrator has secretly held affection for the girl, and, since they are neighbors, he would watch her from afar. Being a shy boy, he dares not speak to her and only professes his love for her in secret.

The day she actually speaks to him is like receiving a call from a goddess. She simply asks him if he is going to Araby, "a splendid bazaar," and mentions that she cannot go because she has to go on a school trip. As a knight before the queen, the narrator promises to bring her back something from the eastern style fair. The rest of the day, he cannot eat, sleep, or study without thinking about her or the promise he made. He asks his aunt and uncle for permission to go to the bazaar, which they give. The rest of the day passes into a blur until he returns from school.

The only problem is he has to wait for his uncle to return from work in order to get money to buy his promised boon, and his uncle is late getting home. As the evening wears on without any sign of his Uncle, the boy endures a torture befitting a questing knight, and he may not even make it to the bazaar before it closes. His uncle finally returns; he had forgotten his promise, and begrudgingly gives the boy money. Racing all the way to the fair, the boy is greeted by a labyrinth of shops. Walking around in such a strange world, he is entranced by the people and the wares. His heart starts to sink when he realizes the great worth of the treasures in the stalls. Before he reaches the middle of the market, the lights go out as the shops close up. The story ends with the narrator recognizing his failure in the quest through grief and irritation. But is our little hero really defeated?

TEXT

North Richmond Street, being blind, was a quiet street except at the hour when the Christian Brothers' School set the boys free. An uninhabited house of two storeys stood at the blind end, detached from its neighbours in a square ground. The other houses of the street, conscious of decent lives within them, gazed at one another with brown imperturbable faces.

The former tenant of our house, a priest, had died in the back drawing-room. Air, musty from having been long enclosed, hung in all the rooms, and the waste room behind the kitchen was littered with old useless papers. Among these I found a few paper-covered books, the pages of which were curled and damp: The Abbot, by Walter Scott, *The Devout Communicant*, and *The Memoirs of Vidocq*. I liked the last best because its leaves were yellow. The wild garden behind the house contained a central apple-tree and a few straggling bushes, under one of which I found the late tenant's rusty bicycle-pump. He had been a very charitable priest; in his will he had left all his money to institutions and the furniture of his house to his sister.

When the short days of winter came, dusk fell before we had well eaten our dinners. When we met in the street the houses had grown sombre. The space of sky above us was the colour of ever-changing violet and towards it the lamps of the street lifted their feeble lanterns. The cold air stung us and we played till our bodies glowed. Our shouts echoed in the silent street. The career of our play brought us through the dark muddy lanes behind the houses, where we ran the gauntlet of the rough tribes from the cottages, to the back doors of the dark dripping gardens where odours arose from the ashpits, to the dark odorous stables where a coachman smoothed and combed the horse or shook music from the buckled harness. When we returned to the street, light from the kitchen windows had filled the areas. If my uncle was seen turning the corner, we hid in the shadow until we had seen him safely housed. Or if Mangan's sister came out on the doorstep to call her brother in to his tea, we watched her from our shadow peer up and down the street. We waited to see whether she would remain or go in and, if she remained, we left our shadow and walked up to Mangan's steps resignedly. She was waiting for us, her figure defined by the light from the half-opened door. Her brother always teased her before he obeyed, and I stood by the railings looking at her. Her dress swung as she moved her body, and the soft rope of her hair tossed from side to side.

Every morning I lay on the floor in the front parlour watching her door. The blind was pulled down to within an inch of the sash so that I could not be seen. When she came out on the doorstep my heart leaped. I ran to the hall, seized my books and followed her. I kept her brown figure always in my eye and, when we came near the point at which our ways diverged, I quickened my pace and passed her. This happened morning after morning. I had never spoken to her, except for a few casual words, and yet her name was like a summons to all my foolish blood.

Her image accompanied me even in places the most

hostile to romance. On Saturday evenings when my aunt went marketing I had to go to carry some of the parcels. We walked through the flaring streets, jostled by drunken men and bargaining women, amid the curses of labourers, the shrill litanies of shop-boys who stood on guard by the barrels of pigs' cheeks, the nasal chanting of street-singers, who sang a come-all-you about O'Donovan Rossa, or a ballad about the troubles in our native land. These noises converged in a single sensation of life for me: I imagined that I bore my chalice safely through a throng of foes. Her name sprang to my lips at moments in strange prayers and praises which I myself did not understand. My eyes were often full of tears (I could not tell why) and at times a flood from my heart seemed to pour itself out into my bosom. I thought little of the future. I did not know whether I would ever speak to her or not or, if I spoke to her, how I could tell her of my confused adoration. But my body was like a harp and her words and gestures were like fingers running upon the wires.

One evening I went into the back drawing-room in which the priest had died. It was a dark rainy evening and there was no sound in the house. Through one of the broken panes I heard the rain impinge upon the earth, the fine incessant needles of water playing in the sodden beds. Some distant lamp or lighted window gleamed below me. I was thankful that I could see so little. All my senses seemed to desire to veil themselves and, feeling that I was about to slip from them, I pressed the palms of my hands together until they trembled, murmuring: 'O love! O love!' many times.

At last she spoke to me. When she addressed the first words to me I was so confused that I did not know what to answer. She asked me was I going to Araby. I forgot whether I answered yes or no. It would be a splendid bazaar; she said she would love to go.

'And why can't you?' I asked.

While she spoke she turned a silver bracelet round and round her wrist. She could not go, she said, because there would be a retreat that week in her convent. Her brother and two other boys were fighting for their caps, and I was alone at the railings. She held one of the spikes, bowing her head towards me. The light from the lamp opposite our door caught the white curve of her neck, lit up her hair that rested there and, falling, lit up the hand upon the railing. It fell over one side of her dress and caught the white border of a petticoat, just visible as she stood at ease.

'It's well for you,' she said.

'If I go,' I said, 'I will bring you something.'

What innumerable follies laid waste my waking and sleeping thoughts after that evening! I wished to annihilate the tedious intervening days. I chafed against the work of school. At night in my bedroom and by day in the classroom her image came between me and the page I strove to read. The syllables of the word Araby were called to me through the silence in which my soul luxuriated and cast an Eastern enchantment over me. I asked for leave to go to the bazaar on Saturday night. My aunt was surprised, and hoped it was not some Freemason affair. I answered few questions in class. I watched my master's face pass from amiability to sternness; he hoped I was not beginning to idle. I could not call my wandering thoughts together. I had hardly any patience with the serious work of life which, now that it stood between me and my desire, seemed to me child's play, ugly monotonous child's play.

On Saturday morning I reminded my uncle that I wished to go to the bazaar in the evening. He was fussing at the hallstand, looking for the hat-brush, and answered me curtly:

'Yes, boy, I know.'

As he was in the hall I could not go into the front parlour and lie at the window. I felt the house in bad humour and walked slowly towards the school. The air was pitilessly raw and already my heart misgave me.

When I came home to dinner my uncle had not yet been home. Still it was early. I sat staring at the clock for some time and, when its ticking began to irritate me, I left the room. I mounted the staircase and gained the upper part of the house. The high, cold, empty, gloomy rooms liberated me and I went from room to room singing. From the front window I saw my companions playing below in the street. Their cries reached me weakened and indistinct and, leaning my forehead against the cool glass, I looked over at the dark house where she lived. I may have stood there for an hour, seeing nothing but the brown-clad figure cast by my imagination, touched discreetly by the lamplight at the curved neck, at the hand upon the railings and at the border below the dress.

When I came downstairs again I found Mrs Mercer sitting at the fire. She was an old, garrulous woman, a pawnbroker's widow, who collected used stamps for some pious purpose. I had to endure the gossip of the tea-table. The meal was prolonged beyond an hour and still my uncle did not come. Mrs. Mercer stood up to go: she was sorry she couldn't wait any longer, but it was after eight o'clock and she did not like to be out late, as the night air was bad for her. When she had gone I began to walk up and down the room, clenching my fists. My aunt said:

'I'm afraid you may put off your bazaar for this night of Our Lord.'

At nine o'clock I heard my uncle's latchkey in the hall door. I heard him talking to himself and heard the hallstand rocking when it had received the weight of his overcoat. I could interpret these signs. When he was midway through his dinner I asked him to give me the money to go to the bazaar. He had forgotten.

'The people are in bed and after their first sleep now,' he said.

I did not smile. My aunt said to him energetically:

'Can't you give him the money and let him go? You've kept him late enough as it is.'

My uncle said he was very sorry he had forgotten. He said he believed in the old saying: 'All work and no play makes Jack a dull boy.' He asked me where I was going and, when I told him a second time, he asked me did I know The Arab's Farewell to his Steed. When I left the kitchen he was about to recite the opening lines of the piece to my aunt.

I held a florin tightly in my hand as I strode down

Buckingham Street towards the station. The sight of the streets thronged with buyers and glaring with gas recalled to me the purpose of my journey. I took my seat in a third-class carriage of a deserted train. After an intolerable delay the train moved out of the station slowly. It crept onward among ruinous houses and over the twinkling river. At Westland Row Station a crowd of people pressed to the carriage doors; but the porters moved them back, saying that it was a special train for the bazaar. I remained alone in the bare carriage. In a few minutes the train drew up beside an improvised wooden platform. I passed out on to the road and saw by the lighted dial of a clock that it was ten minutes to ten. In front of me was a large building which displayed the magical name.

I could not find any sixpenny entrance and, fearing that the bazaar would be closed, I passed in quickly through a turnstile, handing a shilling to a weary-looking man. I found myself in a big hall girded at half its height by a gallery. Nearly all the stalls were closed and the greater part of the hall was in darkness. I recognized a silence like that which pervades a church after a service. I walked into the centre of the bazaar timidly. A few people were gathered about the stalls which were still open. Before a curtain, over which the words Café Chantant were written in coloured lamps, two men were counting money on a salver. I listened to the fall of the coins.

Remembering with difficulty why I had come, I went over to one of the stalls and examined porcelain vases and flowered tea-sets. At the door of the stall a young lady was talking and laughing with two young gentlemen. I remarked their English accents and listened vaguely to their conversation.

'O, I never said such a thing!'

'O, but you did!'

'O, but I didn't!'

'Didn't she say that?'

'Yes. I heard her.'

'O, there's a... fib!'

Observing me, the young lady came over and asked me did I wish to buy anything. The tone of her voice was not encouraging; she seemed to have spoken to me out of a sense of duty. I looked humbly at the great jars that stood like eastern guards at either side of the dark entrance to the stall and murmured:

'No, thank you.'

The young lady changed the position of one of the vases and went back to the two young men. They began to talk of the same subject. Once or twice the young lady glanced at me over her shoulder.

I lingered before her stall, though I knew my stay was useless, to make my interest in her wares seem the more real. Then I turned away slowly and walked down the middle of the bazaar. I allowed the two pennies to fall against the sixpence in my pocket. I heard a voice call from one end of the gallery that the light was out. The upper part of the hall was now completely dark.

Gazing up into the darkness I saw myself as a creature driven and derided by vanity; and my eyes burned with anguish and anger.

EXPLANATION OF
Words & Idioms

Amiability: (adj) friendly and likeable.

Ashpit: (n) a hole beneath a fireplace where the ashes fall; an ash-hole.

Bazaar: (n) an outdoor market with shops and stalls along the street.

Chafed: (v) to become annoyed.

Convent: (n) a church or building where nuns live.

Deride: (v) mock, make fun of.

Drawing-room: (n) a room in a house where a group goes to after a dinner to smoke and talk.

Florin: (n) a British coin worth two shillings (see shilling).

Folly: (v) to do something foolish usually with a negative outcome.

Garrulous: (adj) talkative; always talking without stopping.

Gauntlet: (n) a difficult trial or ordeal.

Hallstand: (n) a piece of furniture in the hallway where hats, coats, and umbrellas are hung.

Harness: (n) gear that is strapped to horse to pull a carriage.

Humour: (n) an old fashioned British word for feeling or mood.

Imperturbable: (adj) calm, unable to be excited.

Impinge: (v) to collide or hit.

Incessant: (adj) continuous without pause.

Litany: (n) a chant or a song that is continuous.
Luxuriate: (v) to spoil oneself.
Odorous: (adj) having a particular smell.
Parlour: (n) a room in a house where people can sit and relax.
Pawnbroker: (n) a person that lends money in exchange for personal property.
Pervade: (v) to exist in the surrounding area.
Petticoat: (n) a female underskirt usually trimmed with lace.
Pious: (adj) religious.
Resignedly: (adv) with a feeling of giving up.
Run the gauntlet: to go through a difficult maze that is often full of danger.
Salver: (n) a tray.
Sash: (n) a window frame
Shilling: (n) A British coin worth one twentieth of a pound, 5 new pence, or 12 old pence prior to 1971.
Sixpenny: (adj) cheap.
Sodden: (adj) to be completely wet.
Sombre: (adj) dark and gloomy.
Tenant: (n) a person that lives a house or apartment.
The Arab's Farewell to his Steed: a short story by Caroline Norton (1808-1887).
Vidocq: the legendary French Detective, not fictitious.

Study Questions

1. How is this story like the quest of a knight? What are the trials he must endure to reach his goal?

2. What kind of a person is the narrator? Though his age is not given, how old do you think he is?

3. What purpose does the use of light serve in the character description of Mangan's sister?

4. What role does the Uncle play in the story?

5. Does the boy hold real love for Mangan's sister, or is it just an infatuation? Use evidence from the story to explain your answer.

6. Is there anything heroic about the narrator? What is or is not heroic about him?

7. The story has great setting descriptions that help us to see the narrator's world. What are some images that stick out in your mind? Why are these so memorable?

8. Is this a light or dark story? Is the boy successful in his journey? Even if he does not gain the "treasure" for Mangan's sister, does he gain anything else? If so, what is it?

9. If the narrator is so fond of Managan's sister, why doesn't he ever mention her name? What does this tell us about his "love" for her?

III. THE STORY OF AN HOUR

by Kate Chopin

Author

Synopsis

Text

Words & Idioms

Story Questions

INTRODUCTION OF THE AUTHOR:
Kate Chopin (1850-1904)

Catherine O'Flaherty was born on July 12, 1850 in St. Louis, Missouri, the youngest of three to an immigrant Irishman, Thomas O'Flaherty and a French-American mother, Eliza Faris. With the death of her father in 1855, Kate found herself living with a widowed mother, grandmother, and great-grandmother, all who were smart, independent women. That same year she entered the Sacred Heart Academy, a Catholic boarding school known for highly intelligent nuns, where she found a love for books, especially the writings of Sir Walter Scott and Charles Dickens. By the time she was thirteen, she decided to drop out of traditional school entirely and devote her own education to books. Such independence lasted only two years, when she decided to return to Sacred Heart Academy. She graduated at the top of her class with a penchant for superb story telling.

In 1870, she married Oscar Chopin, who was a fair man of liberal thinking and afforded his new wife all the luxuries and freedom an intelligent, independent woman could want. She was even known to walk through the city streets unaccompanied by her husband, which caused quite a stir amongst the locals. Oscar bought a cotton plantation, which he didn't manage very effectively. By they time she was 28, she gave birth to five boys and two girls. Four years later Oscar died of swamp fever, leaving his widow and seven kids in considerable debt. Selling the plantation, Kate moved in with her mother, only to see her die the next year. Forced to alternative means of making money, Kate turned to writing, where she set her pen to the lifestyle and people she knew in Louisiana. She published her first novel, *At Fault*, in 1890 but had already started her writing career the previous year with the publication of three short stories. "The Story of an Hour," perhaps her most anthologized short story, was published in 1891. The focus of independent women in these stories shut editors off from her work and she was forced to pay for the publication of her first novel out of her own pocket.

Her highest critical acclaim came in 1894, with the publication of a collection of short stories in *Bayou Folk* that showcased the classical Chopin characters of self-reliant women struggling for purpose in a male dominated society. She followed the success of her first collection with a second in 1897, *A Night in Acadia*. Yet it is with her most respected novel to date that nearly ruined her career. *The Awakening*, published in 1899, marked the turning point of her literary career by proving that she was a novelist worthy of remembrance; it is considered an American masterpiece now, but also ended her critical reputation and career as a writer. America at the time was not yet ready for the strong feminist viewpoint of Chopin or her novel's protagonist, Edna Pontellier, who "awakens" into the full independency and sexuality of womanhood that is applauded by readers today. The critical backlash surprised Chopin, which hurt her deeply, causing her to destroy the manuscript, and over the next five years, she only published a couple of short stories that were not paid much attention to.

Five years after her dismal failure, Kate Chopin died,

forgotten and resentful, from a brain hemorrhage in 1904. Though her critics had managed to destroy her literary life, and her contemporary fans had abandoned her, Chopin found renewed interest in the 1960's as the leading feminist voice of her time.

Synopsis

Mrs. Mallard, a typical Victorian woman, oppressed and emotionally tied to her husband, is suffering from a heart condition. Upon learning that her husband has died in a train crash, Mrs. Mallard confines herself to her room to properly mourn the passing of her husband. Upon deeper contemplation, she soon starts to see that her life isn't over now that her husband has passed, but is, in fact, just beginning; she is now free. Finding the strength and the will to continue on as an "independent" woman, Ms. Mallard now emerges from isolation. Upon her descent down the stairs, she notices someone entering the house. It is none other than Mr. Mallard; the sight of which causes the heart of poor Mrs. Mallard to stop, killing her. Though all who witness this unfortunate event conclude that Mrs. Mallard has died from the joy of her husband's return, the reader sees the irony of his return; she dies not from joy, but from the shock of loosing her newly found life.

TEXT

Knowing that Mrs. Mallard was afflicted with a heart trouble, great care was taken to break to her as gently as possible the news of her husband's death.

It was her sister Josephine who told her, in broken sentences; veiled hints that revealed in half concealing. Her husband's friend Richards was there, too, near her. It was he who had been in the newspaper office when intelligence of the railroad disaster was received, with Brently Mallard's name leading the list of "killed." He had only taken the time to assure himself of its truth by a second telegram, and had hastened to forestall any less careful, less tender friend in bearing the sad message.

She did not hear the story as many women have heard the same, with a paralyzed inability to accept its significance. She wept at once, with sudden, wild abandonment, in her sister's arms. When the storm of grief had spent itself she went away to her room alone. She would have no one follow her.

There stood, facing the open window, a comfortable, roomy armchair. Into this she sank, pressed down by a physical exhaustion that haunted her body and seemed to reach into her soul.

She could see in the open square before her house the tops of trees that were all aquiver with the new spring life. The delicious breath of rain was in the air. In the street below a peddler was crying his wares. The notes of a distant song, which someone was singing, reached her faintly, and countless sparrows were twittering in the eaves.

There were patches of blue sky showing here and there through the clouds that had met and piled one above the other in the west facing her window.

She sat with her head thrown back upon the cushion of the chair, quite motionless, except when a sob came up into her throat and shook her, as a child who has cried itself to sleep continues to sob in its dreams.

She was young, with a fair, calm face, whose lines bespoke repression and even a certain strength. But now there was a dull stare in her eyes, whose gaze was fixed away off yonder on one of those patches of blue sky. It was not a glance of reflection, but rather indicated a suspension of intelligent thought.

There was something coming to her and she was waiting for it, fearfully. What was it? She did not know; it was too subtle and elusive to name. But she felt it, creeping out of the sky, reaching toward her through the sounds, the scents, the color that filled the air.

Now her bosom rose and fell tumultuously. She was beginning to recognize this thing that was approaching to possess her, and she was striving to beat it back with her will □ as powerless as her two white slender hands would have been.

When she abandoned herself a little whispered word escaped her slightly parted lips. She said it over and over under her breath: "free, free, free!" The vacant stare and the look of terror that had followed it went from her eyes. They stayed keen and bright. Her pulses beat fast, and the coursing blood warmed and relaxed every inch of her body.

She did not stop to ask if it were or were not a monstrous joy that held her. A clear and exalted perception enabled her to dismiss the suggestion as trivial.

She knew that she would weep again when she saw the kind, tender hands folded in death; the face that had never looked save with love upon her, fixed and gray and dead. But she saw beyond that bitter moment a long procession of years to come that would belong to her absolutely. And she opened and spread her arms out to them in welcome.

There would be no one to live for during those coming years; she would live for herself. There would be no powerful will bending hers in that blind persistence with which men and women believe they have a right to impose a private will upon a fellow-creature. A kind intention or a cruel intention made the act seem no less a crime as she looked upon it in that brief moment of illumination.

And yet she had loved him □ sometimes. Often she had not. What did it matter! What could love, the unsolved mystery, count for in face of this possession of self-assertion which she suddenly recognized as the strongest impulse of her being!

"Free! Body and soul free!" she kept whispering.

Josephine was kneeling before the closed door with her lips to the keyhole, imploring for admission. "Louise, open the door! I beg, open the door □ you will make yourself ill. What are you doing Louise? For heaven's sake open the door."

"Go away. I am not making myself ill." No; she was drinking in a very elixir of life through that open window.

Her fancy was running riot along those days ahead of her. Spring days, and summer days, and all sorts of days that would be her own. She breathed a quick prayer that life might be long. It was only yesterday she had thought with a shudder that life might be long.

She arose at length and opened the door to her sister's importunities. There was a feverish triumph in her eyes, and she carried herself unwittingly like a goddess of Victory. She clasped her sister's waist, and together they descended the stairs. Richards stood waiting for them at the bottom.

Some one was opening the front door with a latchkey. It was Brently Mallard who entered, a little travel-stained, composedly carrying his grip-sack and umbrella. He had been far from the scene of accident, and did not even know there had been one. He stood amazed at Josephine's piercing cry; at Richards' quick motion to screen him from the view of his wife.

But Richards was too late.

When the doctors came they said she had died of heart disease □ of joy that kills.

EXPLANATION OF
Words & Idioms

Afflicted: (adj) troubled with physical suffering, especially a disease.

Aquiver: (adj) shaking or trembling.

Bespeak: (v) to show or indicate.

Course: (v) to move quickly or pump.

Elixir: (n) a medicinal cure for all ills.

Forestall: (v) to delay.

Grip-sack: (n) a small travel case.

Importunity: (n) a constant, nagging request.

Impose: (v) to force.

Keen: (adj) sharp and bright.

Repression: (n) the state of controlling something by force.

Self-assertion: (n) positive development of one's own behavior.

Subtle: (adj) small or difficult to comprehend.

Telegram: (n) a message received by a telegraph (the sending and receiving of electrical signals by wire), often before the invention of the telephone.

Tumultuously: (adv) in a violent or forced manner.

Twittering: (v) the chirping sound a bird makes; chirruping.

Veiled: (adj) hidden.

Study Questions

1. The first thing that we read about Mrs. Mallard is that she has heart trouble, and other people respond to her according to this condition. How might heart trouble be more than a physical illness? Evidently this seems to be an important part of who she is. So who do you think took care to break her the news of her husband's death?

2. Why is this story written in the passive voice, with a hidden narrator? Why is there a secondary narrator? Was the narrator present at the time of this incident or is the narrator telling a second-hand tale?

3. What are the clues in the story that the Mrs. Mallard's physical and mental condition is connected? How does this clue us into what will happen at the end of the story?

4. Look for repeated uses of the negatives and positives in the story. What are some examples of these? Why are positives and negatives used in this way? What is the purpose they play in this story?

5. The story is short, but we get rich details as to what kind of woman Mrs. Mallard is. What sort of person is she? Is this a positive or a negative portrayal of her? Give examples to support your answer.

6. What is Mrs. Mallard's, or possibly Kate Chopin's, general view of relationships between men and women? Do you agree with this view? Why or why not?

7. We get only a brief but accurate description of the husband: "It was Brently Mallard who entered, a little travel-stained, composedly carrying his grip-sack and umbrella." If he was not on the train, then why is he stained by travel? This is our main picture of him; does it go beyond the state of his clothing? It is a "grip-sack," not a "briefcase" or "suitcase"; what does this word suggest (again, given that we have been told almost nothing else about him)? Does his distance echo, in figurative terms, the nature of their marriage?

8. Mrs. Mallard dies from "the joy that kills." Whose interests does this diagnosis serve? How is it reflective of Chopin's implied view of marriage?

IV. THE YELLOW WALLPAPER

by Charlotte Perkins Gilman

Author

Synopsis

Text

Words & Idioms

Story Questions

INTRODUCTION OF THE AUTHOR:
Charlotte Perkins Gilman (1860-1935)

As one of the prominent feminists at the beginning of the twentieth century, Charlotte Perkins Gilman knew first hand the damage caused by the bigotry of the ruling male class. In 1884, Charlotte suffered from postpartum depression that followed the birth of her daughter, and as the protagonist in her most widely read short story, "The Yellow Wallpaper" (1892), a "specialist" confined her to bed with orders not to exert herself physically or mentally, all of which almost destroyed her sanity. Born on July 3, 1860, Charlotte's father was known to disappear for great lengths of time, which caused Charlotte to live with her great Aunt Harriet Beecher Stowe, who wrote the abolitionist novel *Uncle Tom's Cabin.* Wishing to bring awareness to the plight of women as Harriet did to the abuses of slavery, Charlotte wrote prolifically on behalf of women's rights, producing thousands of works from poems to novels. In 1890, she started to make a name for herself by lecturing around the country on women's rights, and that women and men should share equally in household chores. She published her first novel, *In This Our World,* in 1893 and from 1909 to 1916 ran her own monthly journal the *Forerunner,* which allowed her to publish many of her own articles and lectures.

After her bought with depression, she divorced, left her daughter in her husband's care, and moved to California where she turned to writing to make a living. Among her works of fiction and poetry, she became best known for her non-fiction, *Women and Economics* (1898) being the most famous of all her works. Thanks to this work, Charlotte became internationally recognized and financially secure. Though she had sworn to never marry after her father abandoned her family, Charlotte entered into her second marriage in 1900 with her first cousin, Houghton Gilman. She remained married until 1932, when she contracted an incurable form of breast cancer. She committed suicide by overdosing on chloroform, which she inhaled. In her suicide note, she wrote of preferring to die by her own hand than through the debilitating illness of cancer.

Synopsis

The narrator, a well-to-do woman with a husband physician, finds herself at a summer home where she must confine herself to her room and not participate in any physical or mental strain. She is constantly at odds with her husband who insists that nothing is really wrong with her, except "temporary nervous depression." The bed cure assigned to her is actually what is making her sicker and sicker. Since she has given birth recently, she is seen to be suffering from postpartum depression, which the author also suffered from.

The narrator decides to record her inner most thoughts and feelings in a journal as a type of therapy to overcome her boredom. She does so in secret, for if her dictatorial husband found out, he would be furious, insinuating that such mental activities from a woman was most surely the cause of her illness, which he says she does not have! The room she is confined to is decorated with musty yellow wallpaper with intricate line patterns. The more she stares at the wallpaper, the more, she insists in her journal, that she can see an actual person moving about behind the pattern. Such a revelation, no doubt, distresses the narrator, and when she relates her various visions, the husband blames her visions on silly feminine imaginations. Though her husband speaks of his love and caring intentions, he obviously does not show it, for the narrator always speaks of feeling utterly alone.

As the days drag on, the woman trapped behind the yellow wallpaper becomes more active and more recognizable. Her husband starts to notice her increasing illness and blames it upon her overactive imagination and not to the simple confinement to her room, or the fact that he makes each and every decision for her. She finally resolves to solve the mystery of the woman in the wallpaper. This gives her a renewed purpose and actually makes her husband feel she is recuperating. While her mind slowly slips into insanity, she feels more and more liberated as the woman in the wallpaper finally escapes. The narrator's husband and servants find her creeping around her room in circles, the paper ripped off the walls, her insanity pushed beyond the limit.

TEXT

It is very seldom that mere ordinary people like John and myself secure ancestral halls for the summer.

A colonial mansion, a hereditary estate, I would say a haunted house, and reach the height of romantic felicity □ but that would be asking too much of fate!

Still I will proudly declare that there is something queer about it.

Else, why should it be let so cheaply? And why have stood so long untenanted?

John laughs at me, of course, but one expects that in marriage.

John is practical in the extreme. He has no patience with faith, an intense horror of superstition, and he scoffs openly at any talk of things not to be felt and seen and put down in figures.

John is a physician, and perhaps □ (I would not say it to a living soul, of course, but this is dead paper and a great relief to my mind) □ perhaps that is one reason I do not get well faster.

You see he does not believe I am sick!

And what can one do?

If a physician of high standing, and one's own husband, assures friends and relatives that there is really nothing the matter with one but temporary nervous depression □ a slight hysterical tendency □ what is one to do?

My brother is also a physician, and also of high standing, and he says the same thing.

So I take phosphates or phosphates □ whichever it is, and tonics, and journeys, and air, and exercise, and am absolutely forbidden to "work" until I am well again.

Personally, I disagree with their ideas.

Personally, I believe that congenial work, with excitement and change, would do me good.

But what is one to do?

I did write for a while in spite of them; but it does exhaust me a good deal □ having to be so sly about it, or else meet with heavy opposition.

I sometimes fancy that in my condition if I had less opposition and more society and stimulus □ but John says the very worst thing I can do is to think about my condition, and I confess it always makes me feel bad.

So I will let it alone and talk about the house.

The most beautiful place! It is quite alone, standing well back from the road, quite three miles from the village. It makes me think of English places that you read about, for there are hedges and walls and gates that lock, and lots of separate little houses for the gardeners and people.

There is a delicious garden! I never saw such a garden □ large and shady, full of box-bordered paths, and lined with long grape-covered arbors with seats under them.

There were greenhouses, too, but they are all broken now.

There was some legal trouble, I believe, something about the heirs and co-heirs; anyhow, the place has been empty for years.

That spoils my ghostliness, I am afraid, but I don't care □ there is something strange about the house □ I can feel it.

I even said so to John one moonlight evening, but he said what I felt was a draught, and shut the window.

I get unreasonably angry with John sometimes. I'm sure I never used to be so sensitive. I think it is due to this nervous condition.

But John says if I feel so, I shall neglect proper self-control; so I take pains to control myself □ before him, at least, and that makes me very tired.

I don't like our room a bit. I wanted one downstairs that opened on the piazza and had roses all over the window, and such pretty old-fashioned chintz hangings! but John would not hear of it.

He said there was only one window and not room for two beds, and no near room for him if he took another.

He is very careful and loving, and hardly lets me stir without special direction.

I have a schedule prescription for each hour in the day; he takes all care from me, and so I feel basely ungrateful not to value it more.

He said we came here solely on my account, that I was to have perfect rest and all the air I could get. "Your exercise depends on your strength, my dear," said he, "and your food somewhat on your appetite; but air you can absorb all the time." So we took the nursery at the top of the house.

It is a big, airy room, the whole floor nearly, with windows that look all ways, and air and sunshine galore. It was nursery first and then playroom and gymnasium, I should judge; for the windows are barred for little children, and there are rings and things in the walls.

The paint and paper look as if a boys' school had used it.

It is stripped off □ the paper □ in great patches all around the head of my bed, about as far as I can reach, and in a great place on the other side of the room low down. I never saw a worse paper in my life.

One of those sprawling flamboyant patterns committing every artistic sin.

It is dull enough to confuse the eye in following, pronounced enough to constantly irritate and provoke study, and when you follow the lame uncertain curves for a little distance they suddenly commit suicide □ plunge off at outrageous angles, destroy themselves in unheard of contradictions.

The color is repellent, almost revolting; a smouldering unclean yellow, strangely faded by the slow-turning sunlight.

It is a dull yet lurid orange in some places, a sickly sulphur tint in others.

No wonder the children hated it! I should hate it myself if I had to live in this room long.

There comes John, and I must put this away, □ he hates to have me write a word.

We have been here two weeks, and I haven't felt like writing before, since that first day.

I am sitting by the window now, up in this atrocious nursery, and there is nothing to hinder my writing as much as I please, save lack of strength.

John is away all day, and even some nights when his cases are serious.

I am glad my case is not serious!

But these nervous troubles are dreadfully depressing.

John does not know how much I really suffer. He knows there is no reason to suffer, and that satisfies him.

Of course it is only nervousness. It does weigh on me so not to do my duty in any way!

I meant to be such a help to John, such a real rest and comfort, and here I am a comparative burden already!

Nobody would believe what an effort it is to do what little I am able, □ to dress and entertain, and order things.

It is fortunate Mary is so good with the baby. Such a dear baby!

And yet I cannot be with him, it makes me so nervous.

I suppose John never was nervous in his life. He laughs at me so about this wall-paper!

At first he meant to repaper the room, but afterwards he said that I was letting it get the better of me, and that nothing was worse for a nervous patient than to give way to such fancies.

He said that after the wall-paper was changed it would be the heavy bedstead, and then the barred windows, and then that gate at the head of the stairs, and so on.

"You know the place is doing you good," he said, "and really, dear, I don't care to renovate the house just for a three months' rental."

"Then do let us go downstairs," I said, "there are such pretty rooms there."

Then he took me in his arms and called me a blessed little goose, and said he would go down cellar, if I wished, and have it whitewashed into the bargain.

But he is right enough about the beds and windows and things.

It is an airy and comfortable room as any one need wish, and, of course, I would not be so silly as to make him uncomfortable just for a whim.

I'm really getting quite fond of the big room, all but that horrid paper.

Out of one window I can see the garden, those mysterious deep-shaded arbors, the riotous old-fashioned flowers, and bushes and gnarly trees.

Out of another I get a lovely view of the bay and a little private wharf belonging to the estate. There is a beautiful shaded lane that runs down there from the house. I always fancy I see people walking in these numerous paths and arbors, but John has cautioned me not to give way to fancy in the least. He says that with my imaginative power and habit of story-making, a nervous weakness like mine is sure to lead to all manner of excited fancies, and that I ought to use my will and good sense to check the tendency. So I try.

I think sometimes that if I were only well enough to write a little it would relieve the press of ideas and rest me.

But I find I get pretty tired when I try.

It is so discouraging not to have any advice and companionship about my work. When I get really well, John says we will ask Cousin Henry and Julia down for a long visit; but he says he would as soon put fireworks in my pillow-case as to let me have those stimulating people about now.

I wish I could get well faster.

But I must not think about that. This paper looks to me as if it knew what a vicious influence it had!

There is a recurrent spot where the pattern lolls like a broken neck and two bulbous eyes stare at you upside down.

I get positively angry with the impertinence of it and the everlastingness. Up and down and sideways they crawl, and those absurd, unblinking eyes are everywhere. There is one place where two breadths didn't match, and the eyes go all up and down the line, one a little higher than the other.

I never saw so much expression in an inanimate thing before, and we all know how much expression they have! I used to lie awake as a child and get more entertainment and terror out of blank walls and plain furniture than most children could find in a toy-store.

I remember what a kindly wink the knobs of our big, old bureau used to have, and there was one chair that always seemed like a strong friend.

I used to feel that if any of the other things looked too fierce I could always hop into that chair and be safe.

The furniture in this room is no worse than inharmonious, however, for we had to bring it all from downstairs. I suppose when this was used as a playroom they had to take the nursery things out, and no wonder! I never saw such ravages as the children have made here.

The wall-paper, as I said before, is torn off in spots, and it sticketh closer than a brother □ they must have had perseverance as well as hatred.

Then the floor is scratched and gouged and splintered, the plaster itself is dug out here and there, and this great heavy bed which is all we found in the room, looks as if it had been through the wars.

But I don't mind it a bit □ only the paper.

There comes John's sister. Such a dear girl as she is, and so careful of me! I must not let her find me writing.

She is a perfect and enthusiastic housekeeper, and hopes for no better profession. I verily believe she thinks it is the writing which made me sick!

But I can write when she is out, and see her a long way off from these windows.

There is one that commands the road, a lovely shaded winding road, and one that just looks off over the country. A lovely country, too, full of great elms and velvet meadows.

This wallpaper has a kind of sub-pattern in a different shade, a particularly irritating one, for you can only see it in certain lights, and not clearly then.

But in the places where it isn't faded and where the sun is just so □ I can see a strange, provoking, formless sort of figure, that seems to skulk about behind that silly and conspicuous front design.

There's sister on the stairs!

Well, the Fourth of July is over! The people are all gone and I am tired out. John thought it might do me good to see a little company, so we just had mother and Nellie and the children down for a week.

Of course I didn't do a thing. Jennie sees to everything now.

But it tired me all the same.

John says if I don't pick up faster he shall send me to Weir Mitchell in the fall.

But I don't want to go there at all. I had a friend who was in his hands once, and she says he is just like John and my brother, only more so!

Besides, it is such an undertaking to go so far.

I don't feel as if it was worth while to turn my hand over for anything, and I'm getting dreadfully fretful and querulous.

I cry at nothing, and cry most of the time.

Of course I don't when John is here, or anybody else, but when I am alone.

And I am alone a good deal just now. John is kept in town very often by serious cases, and Jennie is good and lets me alone when I want her to.

So I walk a little in the garden or down that lovely lane, sit on the porch under the roses, and lie down up here a good deal.

I'm getting really fond of the room in spite of the wallpaper. Perhaps because of the wallpaper.

It dwells in my mind so!

I lie here on this great immovable bed □ it is nailed down, I believe □ and follow that pattern about by the hour. It is as good as gymnastics, I assure you. I start, we'll say, at the bottom, down in the corner over there where it has not been touched, and I determine for the thousandth time that I will follow that pointless pattern to some sort of a conclusion.

I know a little of the principle of design, and I know this thing was not arranged on any laws of radiation, or alternation, or repetition, or symmetry, or anything else that I ever heard of.

It is repeated, of course, by the breadths, but not otherwise.

Looked at in one way each breadth stands alone, the bloated curves and flourishes □ a kind of "debased Romanesque" with delirium tremens □ go waddling up and down in isolated columns of fatuity.

But, on the other hand, they connect diagonally, and the sprawling outlines run off in great slanting waves of optic horror, like a lot of wallowing seaweeds in full chase.

The whole thing goes horizontally, too, at least it seems so, and I exhaust myself in trying to distinguish the order of its going in that direction.

They have used a horizontal breadth for a frieze, and that adds wonderfully to the confusion.

There is one end of the room where it is almost intact, and there, when the crosslights fade and the low sun shines directly upon it, I can almost fancy radiation after all, □ the interminable grotesques seem to form around a common centre and rush off in headlong plunges of equal distraction.

It makes me tired to follow it. I will take a nap I guess.

I don't know why I should write this.

I don't want to.

I don't feel able.

And I know John would think it absurd. But I must say what I feel and think in some way □ it is such a relief!

But the effort is getting to be greater than the relief.

Half the time now I am awfully lazy, and lie down ever so much.

John says I mustn't lose my strength, and has me take

cod liver oil and lots of tonics and things, to say nothing of ale and wine and rare meat.

Dear John! He loves me very dearly, and hates to have me sick. I tried to have a real earnest reasonable talk with him the other day, and tell him how I wish he would let me go and make a visit to Cousin Henry and Julia.

But he said I wasn't able to go, nor able to stand it after I got there; and I did not make out a very good case for myself, for I was crying before I had finished.

It is getting to be a great effort for me to think straight. Just this nervous weakness I suppose.

And dear John gathered me up in his arms, and just carried me upstairs and laid me on the bed, and sat by me and read to me till it tired my head.

He said I was his darling and his comfort and all he had, and that I must take care of myself for his sake, and keep well.

He says no one but myself can help me out of it, that I must use my will and self-control and not let any silly fancies run away with me.

There's one comfort, the baby is well and happy, and does not have to occupy this nursery with the horrid wallpaper.

If we had not used it, that blessed child would have! What a fortunate escape! Why, I wouldn't have a child of mine, an impressionable little thing, live in such a room for worlds.

I never thought of it before, but it is lucky that John kept me here after all, I can stand it so much easier than a baby, you see.

Of course I never mention it to them any more □ I am too wise, □ but I keep watch of it all the same.

There are things in that paper that nobody knows but me, or ever will.

Behind that outside pattern the dim shapes get clearer every day.

It is always the same shape, only very numerous.

And it is like a woman stooping down and creeping about behind that pattern. I don't like it a bit. I wonder □ I begin to think □ I wish John would take me away from here!

It is so hard to talk to John about my case, because he is so wise, and because he loves me so.

But I tried it last night.

It was moonlight. The moon shines in all around just as the sun does.

I hate to see it sometimes, it creeps so slowly, and always comes in by one window or another.

John was asleep and I hated to waken him, so I kept still and watched the moonlight on that undulating wallpaper till I felt creepy.

The faint figure behind seemed to shake the pattern, just as if she wanted to get out.

I got up softly and went to feel and see if the paper did move, and when I came back John was awake.

"What is it, little girl?" he said. "Don't go walking about like that □ you'll get cold."

I thought it was a good time to talk, so I told him that I really was not gaining here, and that I wished he would take me away.

"Why, darling!" said he, "our lease will be up in three weeks, and I can't see how to leave before.

"The repairs are not done at home, and I cannot possibly leave town just now. Of course if you were in any danger, I could and would, but you really are better, dear, whether you can see it or not. I am a doctor, dear, and I know. You are gaining flesh and color, your appetite is better, I feel really much easier about you."

"I don't weigh a bit more," said I, "nor as much; and my appetite may be better in the evening when you are here, but it is worse in the morning when you are away!"

"Bless her little heart!" said he with a big hug, "she shall be as sick as she pleases! But now let's improve the shining hours by going to sleep, and talk about it in the morning!"

"And you won't go away?" I asked gloomily.

"Why, how can I, dear? It is only three weeks more and then we will take a nice little trip of a few days while Jennie is getting the house ready. Really dear you are better!"

"Better in body perhaps□" I began, and stopped short, for he sat up straight and looked at me with such a stern, reproachful look that I could not say another word.

"My darling," said he, "I beg of you, for my sake and for our child's sake, as well as for your own, that you will never for one instant let that idea enter your mind! There is nothing so dangerous, so fascinating, to a temperament like yours. It is a false and foolish fancy. Can you not trust me as a physician when I tell you so?"

So of course I said no more on that score, and we went to sleep before long. He thought I was asleep first, but I wasn't, and lay there for hours trying to decide whether that front pattern and the back pattern really did move together or separately.

On a pattern like this, by daylight, there is a lack of sequence, a defiance of law, that is a constant irritant to a normal mind.

The color is hideous enough, and unreliable enough, and infuriating enough, but the pattern is torturing.

You think you have mastered it, but just as you get well underway in following, it turns a back-somersault and there you are. It slaps you in the face, knocks you down, and tramples upon you. It is like a bad dream.

The outside pattern is a florid arabesque, reminding one of a fungus. If you can imagine a toadstool in joints, an interminable string of toadstools, budding and sprouting in endless convolutions □ why, that is something like it.

That is, sometimes!

There is one marked peculiarity about this paper, a thing nobody seems to notice but myself, and that is that it changes as the light changes.

When the sun shoots in through the east window □ I always watch for that first long, straight ray □ it changes so quickly that I never can quite believe it.

That is why I watch it always.

By moonlight □ the moon shines in all night when there is a moon □ I wouldn't know it was the same paper.

At night in any kind of light, in twilight, candlelight, lamplight, and worst of all by moonlight, it becomes bars! The outside pattern I mean, and the woman behind it is as plain as can be.

I didn't realize for a long time what the thing was that showed behind, that dim sub-pattern, but now I am quite sure it is a woman.

By daylight she is subdued, quiet. I fancy it is the pattern that keeps her so still. It is so puzzling. It keeps me quiet by the hour.

I lie down ever so much now. John says it is good for me, and to sleep all I can.

Indeed he started the habit by making me lie down for an hour after each meal.

It is a very bad habit I am convinced, for you see I don't sleep.

And that cultivates deceit, for I don't tell them I'm awake □ O no!

The fact is I am getting a little afraid of John.

He seems very queer sometimes, and even Jennie has an inexplicable look.

It strikes me occasionally, just as a scientific hypothesis, □ that perhaps it is the paper!

I have watched John when he did not know I was looking, and come into the room suddenly on the most innocent excuses, and I've caught him several times looking at the paper! And Jennie too. I caught Jennie with her hand on it once.

She didn't know I was in the room, and when I asked her in a quiet, a very quiet voice, with the most restrained manner possible, what she was doing with the paper □ she turned around as if she had been caught stealing, and looked quite angry □ asked me why I should frighten her so!

Then she said that the paper stained everything it

touched, that she had found yellow smooches on all my clothes and John's, and she wished we would be more careful!

Did not that sound innocent? But I know she was studying that pattern, and I am determined that nobody shall find it out but myself!

Life is very much more exciting now than it used to be. You see I have something more to expect, to look forward to, to watch. I really do eat better, and am more quiet than I was.

John is so pleased to see me improve! He laughed a little the other day, and said I seemed to be flourishing in spite of my wall-paper.

I turned it off with a laugh. I had no intention of telling him it was because of the wall-paper □ he would make fun of me. He might even want to take me away.

I don't want to leave now until I have found it out. There is a week more, and I think that will be enough.

I'm feeling ever so much better! I don't sleep much at night, for it is so interesting to watch developments; but I sleep a good deal in the daytime.

In the daytime it is tiresome and perplexing.

There are always new shoots on the fungus, and new shades of yellow all over it. I cannot keep count of them, though I have tried conscientiously.

It is the strangest yellow, that wall-paper! It makes me think of all the yellow things I ever saw □ not beautiful ones like buttercups, but old foul, bad yellow things.

But there is something else about that paper □ the smell! I noticed it the moment we came into the room, but with so much air and sun it was not bad. Now we have had a week of fog and rain, and whether the windows are open or not, the smell is here.

It creeps all over the house.

I find it hovering in the dining-room, skulking in the parlor, hiding in the hall, lying in wait for me on the stairs.

It gets into my hair.

Even when I go to ride, if I turn my head suddenly and surprise it □ there is that smell!

Such a peculiar odor, too! I have spent hours in trying to analyze it, to find what it smelled like.

It is not bad □ at first, and very gentle, but quite the subtlest, most enduring odor I ever met.

In this damp weather it is awful, I wake up in the night and find it hanging over me.

It used to disturb me at first. I thought seriously of burning the house □ to reach the smell.

But now I am used to it. The only thing I can think of that it is like is the color of the paper! A yellow smell.

There is a very funny mark on this wall, low down, near the mopboard. A streak that runs round the room. It goes behind every piece of furniture, except the bed, a long, straight, even smooch, as if it had been rubbed over and over.

I wonder how it was done and who did it, and what they did it for. Round and round and round □ round and round and round □ it makes me dizzy!

I really have discovered something at last.

Through watching so much at night, when it changes so, I have finally found out.

The front pattern does move □ and no wonder! The woman behind shakes it!

Sometimes I think there are a great many women behind, and sometimes only one, and she crawls around fast, and her crawling shakes it all over.

Then in the very bright spots she keeps still, and in the very shady spots she just takes hold of the bars and shakes them hard.

And she is all the time trying to climb through. But nobody could climb through that pattern □ it strangles so; I think that is why it has so many heads.

They get through, and then the pattern strangles them off and turns them upside down, and makes their eyes white!

If those heads were covered or taken off it would not be half so bad.

I think that woman gets out in the daytime!

And I'll tell you why □ privately □ I've seen her!

I can see her out of every one of my windows!

It is the same woman, I know, for she is always creeping, and most women do not creep by daylight.

I see her in that long shaded lane, creeping up and down. I see her in those dark grape arbors, creeping all around the garden.

I see her on that long road under the trees, creeping along, and when a carriage comes she hides under the blackberry vines.

I don't blame her a bit. It must be very humiliating to be caught creeping by daylight!

I always lock the door when I creep by daylight. I can't do

it at night, for I know John would suspect something at once.

And John is so queer now, that I don't want to irritate him. I wish he would take another room! Besides, I don't want anybody to get that woman out at night but myself.

I often wonder if I could see her out of all the windows at once.

But, turn as fast as I can, I can only see out of one at one time.

And though I always see her, she may be able to creep faster than I can turn!

I have watched her sometimes away off in the open country, creeping as fast as a cloud shadow in a high wind.

If only that top pattern could be gotten off from the under one! I mean to try it, little by little.

I have found out another funny thing, but I shan't tell it this time! It does not do to trust people too much.

There are only two more days to get this paper off, and I believe John is beginning to notice. I don't like the look in his eyes.

And I heard him ask Jennie a lot of professional questions about me. She had a very good report to give.

She said I slept a good deal in the daytime.

John knows I don't sleep very well at night, for all I'm so quiet!

He asked me all sorts of questions, too, and pretended to be very loving and kind.

As if I couldn't see through him!

Still, I don't wonder he acts so, sleeping under this paper

for three months.

It only interests me, but I feel sure John and Jennie are secretly affected by it.

Hurrah! This is the last day, but it is enough. John to stay in town over night, and won't be out until this evening.

Jennie wanted to sleep with me □ the sly thing! But I told her I should undoubtedly rest better for a night all alone.

That was clever, for really I wasn't alone a bit! As soon as it was moonlight and that poor thing began to crawl and shake the pattern, I got up and ran to help her.

I pulled and she shook, I shook and she pulled, and before morning we had peeled off yards of that paper.

A strip about as high as my head and half around the room.

And then when the sun came and that awful pattern began to laugh at me, I declared I would finish it today!

We go away tomorrow, and they are moving all my furniture down again to leave things as they were before.

Jennie looked at the wall in amazement, but I told her merrily that I did it out of pure spite at the vicious thing.

She laughed and said she wouldn't mind doing it herself, but I must not get tired.

How she betrayed herself that time!

But I am here, and no person touches this paper but me, □ not alive!

She tried to get me out of the room □ it was too patent! But I said it was so quiet and empty and clean now that I believed I would lie down again and sleep all I could; and not to wake me even for dinner □ I would call when I woke.

So now she is gone, and the servants are gone, and the things are gone, and there is nothing left but that great bedstead nailed down, with the canvas mattress we found on it.

We shall sleep downstairs tonight, and take the boat home tomorrow.

I quite enjoy the room, now it is bare again.

How those children did tear about here!

This bedstead is fairly gnawed!

But I must get to work.

I have locked the door and thrown the key down into the front path.

I don't want to go out, and I don't want to have anybody come in, till John comes.

I want to astonish him.

I've got a rope up here that even Jennie did not find. If that woman does get out, and tries to get away, I can tie her!

But I forgot I could not reach far without anything to stand on!

This bed will not move!

I tried to lift and push it until I was lame, and then I got so angry I bit off a little piece at one corner □ but it hurt my teeth.

Then I peeled off all the paper I could reach standing on the floor. It sticks horribly and the pattern just enjoys it! All those strangled heads and bulbous eyes and waddling fungus growths just shriek with derision!

I am getting angry enough to do something desperate. To jump out of the window would be admirable exercise, but the bars are too strong even to try.

Besides I wouldn't do it. Of course not. I know well enough that a step like that is improper and might be misconstrued.

I don't like to look out of the windows even □ there are so many of those creeping women, and they creep so fast.

I wonder if they all come out of that wall-paper as I did?

But I am securely fastened now by my well-hidden rope □ you don't get me out in the road there!

I suppose I shall have to get back behind the pattern when it comes night, and that is hard!

It is so pleasant to be out in this great room and creep around as I please!

I don't want to go outside. I won't, even if Jennie asks me to.

For outside you have to creep on the ground, and everything is green instead of yellow.

But here I can creep smoothly on the floor, and my shoulder just fits in that long smooch around the wall, so I cannot lose my way.

Why there's John at the door!

It is no use, young man, you can't open it!

How he does call and pound!

Now he's crying for an axe.

It would be a shame to break down that beautiful door!

"John dear!" said I in the gentlest voice, "the key is down by the front steps, under a plaintain leaf!"

That silenced him for a few moments.

Then he said □ very quietly indeed, "Open the door, my darling!"

"I can't," said I. "The key is down by the front door under a plantain leaf!"

And then I said it again, several times, very gently and slowly, and said it so often that he had to go and see, and he got it of course, and came in. He stopped short by the door.

"What is the matter?" he cried. "For God's sake, what are you doing! "

I kept on creeping just the same, but I looked at him over my shoulder.

"I've got out at last," said I, "in spite of you and Jane. And I've pulled off most of the paper, so you can't put me back!"

Now why should that man have fainted? But he did, and right across my path by the wall, so that I had to creep over him every time!

EXPLANATION OF
Words & Idioms

Arabesque: (n) an elaborate pattern.

Arbor: (n) a place to rest in a garden or park that offers shade from a latticed wooden wall and top that has vines and other plants growing from it.

Atrocious: (adj) very bad or ugly.

Bulbous: (adj) rounded or swollen.

Chintz: (n) a cotton fabric of bright colors.

Congenial: (adj) appropriate to one's needs.

Convolution: (n) a folded or twisting form.

Debased Romanesque: (n) a low quality style of popular forms and architecture that used large curves and arches in its style.

Delirium tremens: (n) a type of hallucination brought on by overuse of alcohol; a kind of high.

Derision: (n) mocking laughter.

Fatuity: (n) stupidity or foolishness.

Flamboyant: (adj) excessively decorated.

Gnarly: (adj) having lots of tree knots sticking out.

Gnaw: (v) to chew or cut up.

Grotesque: (n) A style of painting or ornamentation with natural forms and monstrous figures entwined in strange or imaginative arrangements.

Impertinence: (n) something that is not relevant or appropriate.

Lurid: (adj) shocking.

Misconstrue: (v) to misunderstand.

Mopboard: (n) baseboard. Molding that runs along the bottom of the wall to protect the wallpaper from getting wet by the mop.

Patent: (adj) obvious.

Phosphate: (n) A salt that comes from phosphoric acid.

Plantain: (n) a large, treelike herb.

Querulous: (adj) whining or always complaining.

Skulk: (v) to hide or prowl.

Smooch: (n) something that has rubbed off onto something else.

Temperament: (n) nature or mood.

Toadstool: (n) an inedible and sometimes poisonous mushroom.

Tonic: (n) a medication that restores strength.

Study Questions

1. How are men portrayed in this story? Is this an accurate portrayal?

2. When does the reader start to see the narrator's mental illness? Was the narrator mentally ill from the beginning or did this happen because of her confinement to the room?

3. How does the husband feel about his wife? Do you think he really loves her? Give specific examples to support your answer.

4. How does the wife feel about her husband? Do you think she really loves him? Give specific examples to support your answer.

5. What is the symbolism behind the wallpaper? Why is it yellow? What significance do the patterns have?

6. What does the woman behind the wallpaper represent? How does the reader's understanding of this woman change throughout the story?

7. Is the ending a happy or tragic ending? Knowing a little about Charlotte Perkins Gilman, could this story be seen as liberation from the confining rule of masculine culture? Why or why not?

8. Do we see the treatment of women with postpartum depression or any other "feminine illness" (i.e. menstruation) as having improved in modern times, or is there still a sense of male perception of "temporary nervous depression" on the part of the woman? Give some examples to back up your answer.

9. How does this story open your perception to the feminist viewpoint? Does it succeed in accuratly describing the plight of 19th century women? Does this story still have significance in the 21st century? How?

V. THE CASK OF AMONTILLADO

by Edgar Allan Poe

INTRODUCTION OF THE AUTHOR:
Edgar Allan Poe (1809-1849)

Judged to be the father of the detective story and of modern horror, Edgar Allan Poe was born January 19, 1809, the son of two poor traveling theater actors; a profession that was not all that esteemed at the time. Edgar's father, David Poe, often appeared drunk on stage and was a notorious drinker and even abandoned his family when Edgar was two years old. A year later his mother died violently of tuberculosis, an event that traumatized him into his later years. Edgar was then taken in by the Allans, though never legally adopted, and given the best education, which included five years in England. Poe entered the University of Virginia where he fell into debt through prodigious gambling, debt which he refused to pay and was thus expelled. His subsequent expulsion from university shamed the Allans deeply upon which they disowned him and even prevented his marriage to Sarah Elmira Royster. Facing a dismal, penniless future, Poe enlisted in the army in 1827, and even wrote poems. His first book of poetry appeared in *Tamerlane and Other Poems*, a style that borrowed heavily from the English poet Lord Byron.

After being honorably discharged from West Point, a top military academy, for refusing to follow orders, Poe turned to writing full time as a contributor to several magazines from 1835 to 1843. During this time, he published some of his best known stories. He moved to Baltimore and lived with his widowed Aunt and her daughter, Virginia Clem. Poe was the center of several scandals when his drinking and drug use became well known. He also caused a stir when he married his 13 year old cousin, Virginia, who died of tuberculosis five years after bursting a blood vessel and becoming an invalid. The drugs and drinking nearly destroyed him after the death of his wife. Poe still maintained legitimacy as a writer as an adept literary critic and by publishing *The Murders in the Rue Morgue* (1841), which became the precursor to the great works of mystery that followed, especially Sir Arthur Conan Doyle's Sherlock Holms character. He also is argued as being the creator of the short story form, though this is still much in debate; his most famous short story being *The Fall of the House of Usher* (1839).

By 1845, Poe had moved to New York where he penned his now famous "The Raven." His erratic behavior and bouts of madness led to his attempting suicide by overdosing on the drug laudanum. It was during this time he penned the supurb tale of cold revenge *The Cask of Amontillado* (1846). Since Poe became associated with tales of the macabre and was well known for being a drug addict and alcoholic, many thought the dark characters of his stories as being somewhat autobiographical. After years of such physical and mental abuse □ the death of his wife, and abject poverty □ Poe was found unconscious in the gutter on October 3, 1849. He stayed in this state for four more days before he died.

Synopsis

The narrator, Montresor, seems upset by all the insults and injuries he has suffered from Fortunato. Though we are never told what these injuries are, or if they are indeed worth the horror he inflicts on Fortunato, Montresor shows that he is cold and calculating in his revenge. Having dismissed all his servants and preparing bricks and mortar in advance, Montresor finds Fortunato at a time of festival and begins to tempt his unwaring prey to following him into the wine cellar beneath his manor where he has stored some very rare wine. He uses reverse psychology to trick Fortunato, who happens to be dressed as a fool for the festival, into following him. Montresor's darkness is even more base as he states concern for Fortunato's health and wellbeing, an obvious lie in light of the way he kills him later.

Giving his prey more liquor to numb his senses, they venture deep within the crypt; and at the farthest reaches, they come to a narrow nook, where he has Fortunato enter to find the rare Amontillado. Inside, Montresor chains him to the wall and starts to trap Fortunato inside by laying bricks in the opening and sealing them with mortar. Fortunato starts to sober to his situation and screams in horror to which Montresor screams back, louder and more insanely until Fortunato becomes quiet. With all but the last brick in place, Fortunato throws the torch in to see the response of his victim and wishes him to rest in peace before sealing the nook, roughly the size of a coffin, forever.

TEXT

The thousand injuries of Fortunato I had borne as I best could, but when he ventured upon insult, I vowed revenge. You, who so well know the nature of my soul, will not suppose, however, that I gave utterance to a threat. AT LENGTH I would be avenged; this was a point definitively settled □ but the very definitiveness with which it was resolved precluded the idea of risk. I must not only punish, but punish with impunity. A wrong is unredressed when retribution overtakes its redresser. It is equally unredressed when the avenger fails to make himself felt as such to him who has done the wrong.

It must be understood that neither by word nor deed had I given Fortunato cause to doubt my good will. I continued as was my wont, to smile in his face, and he did not perceive that my smile NOW was at the thought of his immolation.

He had a weak point □ this Fortunato □ although in other regards he was a man to be respected and even feared. He prided himself on his connoisseurship in wine. Few Italians have the true virtuoso spirit. For the most part their enthusiasm is adopted to suit the time and opportunity to practise imposture upon the British and Austrian MILLIONAIRES. In painting and gemmary, Fortunato, like his countrymen , was a quack, but in the matter of old wines he was sincere. In this respect I did not differ from him materially; I was skilful in the Italian vintages myself, and bought largely whenever I could.

It was about dusk, one evening during the supreme

madness of the carnival season, that I encountered my friend. He accosted me with excessive warmth, for he had been drinking much. The man wore motley. He had on a tight-fitting parti-striped dress and his head was surmounted by the conical cap and bells. I was so pleased to see him, that I thought I should never have done wringing his hand.

I said to him □ "My dear Fortunato, you are luckily met. How remarkably well you are looking today! But I have received a pipe of what passes for Amontillado, and I have my doubts."

"How?" said he, "Amontillado? A pipe? Impossible ? And in the middle of the carnival?"

"I have my doubts," I replied; "and I was silly enough to pay the full Amontillado price without consulting you in the matter. You were not to be found, and I was fearful of losing a bargain."

"Amontillado!"

"I have my doubts."

"Amontillado!"

"And I must satisfy them."

"Amontillado!"

"As you are engaged, I am on my way to Luchesi. If any one has a critical turn, it is he. He will tell me" □

"Luchesi cannot tell Amontillado from Sherry."

"And yet some fools will have it that his taste is a match for your own."

"Come let us go."

"Whither?"

"To your vaults."

"My friend, no; I will not impose upon your good nature. I perceive you have an engagement Luchesi" □

"I have no engagement; come."

"My friend, no. It is not the engagement, but the severe cold with which I perceive you are afflicted. The vaults are insufferably damp. They are encrusted with nitre."

"Let us go, nevertheless. The cold is merely nothing. Amontillado! You have been imposed upon; and as for Luchesi, he cannot distinguish Sherry from Amontillado."

Thus speaking, Fortunato possessed himself of my arm. Putting on a mask of black silk and drawing a roquelaire closely about my person, I suffered him to hurry me to my palazzo.

There were no attendants at home; they had absconded to make merry in honour of the time. I had told them that I should not return until the morning and had given them explicit orders not to stir from the house. These orders were sufficient, I well knew, to insure their immediate disappearance, one and all, as soon as my back was turned.

I took from their sconces two flambeaux, and giving one to Fortunato bowed him through several suites of rooms to the archway that led into the vaults. I passed down a long and winding staircase, requesting him to be cautious as he followed. We came at length to the foot of the descent, and stood together on the damp ground of the catacombs of the Montresors.

The gait of my friend was unsteady, and the bells upon his cap jingled as he strode.

"The pipe," said he.

"It is farther on," said I; "but observe the white webwork which gleams from these cavern walls."

He turned towards me and looked into my eyes with two filmy orbs that distilled the rheum of intoxication .

"Nitre?" he asked, at length

"Nitre," I replied. "How long have you had that cough!"

"Ugh! ugh! ugh! □ ugh! ugh! ugh! □ ugh! ugh! ugh! □ ugh! ugh! ugh! □ ugh! ugh! ugh!

My poor friend found it impossible to reply for many minutes.

"It is nothing," he said, at last.

"Come," I said, with decision, we will go back; your health is precious. You are rich, respected, admired, beloved; you are happy as once I was. You are a man to be missed. For me it is no matter. We will go back; you will be ill and I cannot be responsible. Besides, there is Luchesi" □

"Enough," he said; "the cough is a mere nothing; it will not kill me. I shall not die of a cough."

"True □ true," I replied; "and, indeed, I had no intention of alarming you unnecessarily □ but you should use all proper caution. A draught of this Medoc will defend us from the damps."

Here I knocked off the neck of a bottle which I drew from a long row of its fellows that lay upon the mould.

"Drink," I said, presenting him the wine.

He raised it to his lips with a leer. He paused and nodded to me familiarly, while his bells jingled.

"I drink," he said, "to the buried that repose around us."

"And I to your long life."

He again took my arm and we proceeded.

"These vaults," he said, are extensive."

"The Montresors," I replied, "were a great numerous family."

"I forget your arms."

"A huge human foot d'or, in a field azure; the foot crushes a serpent rampant whose fangs are imbedded in the heel."

"And the motto?"

"Nemo me impune lacessit."

"Good!" he said.

The wine sparkled in his eyes and the bells jingled. My own fancy grew warm with the Medoc. We had passed through walls of piled bones, with casks and puncheons intermingling, into the inmost recesses of the catacombs. I paused again, and this time I made bold to seize Fortunato by an arm above the elbow.

"The nitre!" I said: see it increases. It hangs like moss upon the vaults. We are below the river's bed. The drops of moisture trickle among the bones. Come, we will go back ere it is too late. Your cough" □

"It is nothing" he said; "let us go on. But first, another draught of the Medoc."

I broke and reached him a flagon of De Grave. He emptied it at a breath. His eyes flashed with a fierce light. He laughed and threw the bottle upwards with a gesticulation I did not understand.

I looked at him in surprise. He repeated the movement □ a grotesque one.

"You do not comprehend?" he said.

"Not I," I replied.

"Then you are not of the brotherhood."

"How?"

"You are not of the masons."

"Yes, yes," I said "yes! yes."

"You? Impossible! A mason?"

"A mason," I replied.

"A sign," he said.

"It is this," I answered, producing a trowel from beneath the folds of my roquelaire.

"You jest," he exclaimed, recoiling a few paces. "But let us proceed to the Amontillado."

"Be it so," I said, replacing the tool beneath the cloak, and again offering him my arm. He leaned upon it heavily. We continued our route in search of the Amontillado. We passed through a range of low arches, descended, passed on, and descending again, arrived at a deep crypt, in which the foulness of the air caused our flambeaux rather to glow than flame.

At the most remote end of the crypt there appeared another less spacious. Its walls had been lined with human remains piled to the vault overhead, in the fashion of the great catacombs of Paris. Three sides of this interior crypt were still ornamented in this manner. From the fourth the bones had been thrown down, and lay promiscuously upon the earth, forming at one point a mound of some size. Within the wall thus exposed by the displacing of the bones, we perceived a still interior recess, in depth about four feet, in width three, in height six or seven. It seemed to have been constructed for no especial use in itself, but formed merely the interval between two of the colossal supports of the roof of the catacombs, and was backed by one of their circumscribing walls of solid granite.

It was in vain that Fortunato, uplifting his dull torch, endeavoured to pry into the depths of the recess. Its termination the feeble light did not enable us to see.

"Proceed," I said; "herein is the Amontillado. As for Luchesi" □

"He is an ignoramus," interrupted my friend, as he stepped unsteadily forward, while I followed immediately at his heels. In an instant he had reached the extremity of the niche, and finding his progress arrested by the rock, stood stupidly bewildered. A moment more and I had fettered him to the granite. In its surface were two iron staples, distant from each other about two feet, horizontally. From one of these depended a short chain. from the other a padlock. Throwing the links about his waist, it was but the work of a few seconds to secure it. He was too much astounded to resist. Withdrawing the key I stepped back from the recess.

"Pass your hand," I said, "over the wall; you cannot help feeling the nitre. Indeed it is VERY damp. Once more let me IMPLORE you to return. No? Then I must positively leave you. But I must first render you all the little attentions in my power."

"The Amontillado!" ejaculated my friend, not yet recovered from his astonishment.

"True," I replied; "the Amontillado."

As I said these words I busied myself among the pile of

bones of which I have before spoken. Throwing them aside, I soon uncovered a quantity of building stone and mortar. With these materials and with the aid of my trowel, I began vigorously to wall up the entrance of the niche.

I had scarcely laid the first tier of my masonry when I discovered that the intoxication of Fortunato had in a great measure worn off. The earliest indication I had of this was a low moaning cry from the depth of the recess. It was NOT the cry of a drunken man. There was then a long and obstinate silence. I laid the second tier, and the third, and the fourth; and then I heard the furious vibrations of the chain. The noise lasted for several minutes, during which, that I might hearken to it with the more satisfaction, I ceased my labours and sat down upon the bones. When at last the clanking subsided, I resumed the trowel, and finished without interruption the fifth, the sixth, and the seventh tier. The wall was now nearly upon a level with my breast. I again paused, and holding the flambeaux over the mason-work, threw a few feeble rays upon the figure within.

A succession of loud and shrill screams, bursting suddenly from the throat of the chained form, seemed to thrust me violently back. For a brief moment I hesitated □ I trembled. Unsheathing my rapier, I began to grope with it about the recess; but the thought of an instant reassured me. I placed my hand upon the solid fabric of the catacombs, and felt satisfied. I reapproached the wall. I replied to the yells of him who clamoured. I reechoed □ I aided □ I surpassed them in volume and in strength. I did this, and the clamourer grew still.

It was now midnight, and my task was drawing to a close. I had completed the eighth, the ninth, and the tenth tier. I had finished a portion of the last and the eleventh; there remained but a single stone to be fitted and plastered in. I struggled with its weight; I placed it partially in its destined position. But now there came from out the niche a low laugh that erected the hairs upon my head. It was succeeded by a sad voice, which I had difficulty in recognising as that of the noble Fortunato. The voice said □

"Ha! ha! ha! □ he! he! □ a very good joke indeed □ an excellent jest. We will have many a rich laugh about it at the palazzo □ he! he! he! □ over our wine □ he! he! he!"

"The Amontillado!" I said.

"He! he! he! □ he! he! he! □ yes, the Amontillado. But is it not getting late? Will not they be awaiting us at the palazzo, the Lady Fortunato and the rest? Let us be gone."

"Yes," I said "let us be gone."

"FOR THE LOVE OF GOD, MONTRESOR!"

"Yes," I said, "for the love of God!"

But to these words I hearkened in vain for a reply. I grew impatient. I called aloud □

"Fortunato!"

No answer. I called again □

"Fortunato!"

No answer still. I thrust a torch through the remaining aperture and let it fall within. There came forth in return only a jingling of the bells. My heart grew sick □ on account of the dampness of the catacombs. I hastened to make an end of my labour. I forced the last stone into its position; I plastered it up. Against the new masonry I reerected the old rampart of bones. For the half of a century no mortal has disturbed them.

In pace requiescat!

EXPLANATION OF
Words & Idioms

Abscond: (v) to leave rapidly so as not to be seen.

Accost: (v) to stand close to a person and talk aggressively or without fear.

Amontillado: (n) a dry, sweet wine (sherry) from Spain.

Arms (coat of arms): (n) a family emblem that shows ancestry.

Azure: (adj) the color of blue.

Cask: (n) a wooden barrel that is used to hold beer or wine.

Connoisseurship: (n) a great knowledge or taste for superior things.

Definitiveness: (n) conclusiveness or finality

d'or: (French) gold.

Ejaculate: (v) to speak quickly and suddenly.

Ere: (prep) before.

Flambeaux: (n) a torch that is already lit.

Gemmary: (n) the skill of cutting of gems.

Gesticulation: (n) moving hands for emphasis while speaking; gesturing.

Ignoramus: (n) a person who is ignorant.

Immolation: (n) killing or destruction.

Impunity: (n) to do something without getting caught, punished, or hurt.

In pace requiescat: (Latin) Rest in peace (May his soul not be troubled in death).

Mason: (n) a person that builds with bricks, also a secret order of fraternity.

Medoc: (n) a red wine from Bordeaux France.

Mortar: (n) a special type of cement that is used to stick bricks together when building.

Motley: (n) the multi-colored clothing worn by a court jester or clown in the Middle Ages.

Nemo me impune lacessit: (Latin) No one assails (attacks) me with impunity (without consequence).

Niche: (n) a small closet-like space in opened in a wall.

Nitre: (n) a crystalline salt composed of potassium nitrate (KNO_3) that grows in caves.

Obstinate: (adj) not willing to follow along with popular opinion; stubborn.

Palazzo: (n) Italian for palace or mansion.

Promiscuously: (adv) without any thought or organization; random.

Puncheon: (n) a large cask that can hold up to 454 liters of wine or liquid.

Rampant: (adj) wild or violent.

Rampart: (n) a pile.

Rapier: (n) a sword with a long, narrow two-edged blade.

Repose: (v) to lie dead.

Rheum: (n) the watery mucous that comes from the eyes.

Roquelaire: (n) now spelled roquelaure. A cloak that men wore in the 18th century that clasped around the throat and extended to the knees.

Sconce: (n) a bracket that held torches to the wall.

Tier: (n) a row or level.

Trowel: (n) a tool that masons use to apply mortar to bricks.

Vault: (n) a large cellar or basement with arched walls and ceiling.

Virtuoso: (adj) having great interest in the fine arts.

Study Questions

1. Does Poe ever create any sympathy for Fortunato or are we supposed to only be appaled by Montresor's actions?

2. At the end of the story, Montresor calls Fortunato's name and gets no response. He even feels sickened. Does Montresor succeed in his revenge or is it only an empty gesture?

3. Does Montresor ever show signs of remorse? Or is he just a sociopath?

4. What is the symbolism of burying people alive? Poe uses this image a lot in stories.

5. Is Montresor a reliable narrator? Can we believe everything that he says in this story?

6. Does Fortunato ever show that he is capable of insulting or hurting a person as Montresor says he has?

7. This story was very dark and horrifying at the time of its publication. Does the story horrify or disburb you in any way? Why or why not?

8. Poe was never considered a man of literary taste by his contemporaries. Does this story have any literary merit, or is it just a piece of "pulp fiction"? Explain your answer.

9. At first we don't quite know what Montresor is going to do, at what point do we know? What are some of the clues?

VI. A WICKED WOMAN

by Jack London

INTRODUCTION OF THE AUTHOR:
Jack London (1876-1916)

Born John Griffith Chaney in San Francisco on January 12, 1876, Jack London was raised by his stepfather, John London, whom he took his last name from after his father abandoned him at an early age. By the time he was ten, he read voraciously and frequented the local public library since his family's poverty couldn't afford him any books. Libraries would continue to be his educator after he left school by the ninth grade and became a self-educated man. While still in his teens, Jack traveled extensively around the American frontier as a railroad hobo (he was arrested for vagrancy in New York), a gold prospector, a soldier, a sailor, and even an oyster pirate in the San Francisco Bay. As an oyster pirate he secured more money in a week than he could as a professional writer in an entire year. Since this was an illegal trade, he eventually reformed and worked on the other side of the law as a fish patrol deputy. He learned about socialism during his travels and returned to California as a street orator who passionately supported the socialist ideals as well as women's suffrage. He even ran for mayor of Oakland under the socialist ticket and remained defeated over several elections.

Jack returned to finish high school and graduated before he was twenty; he then entered the University of California, Berkeley, where he only stayed for six months before he left, finding the academic atmosphere rather passionless. You would think that he had found passion with Bess Madern who had been tutoring him in math, and whom he married in 1900, yet it was just a typical Victorian courtship based on circumstance and not love. They did have two children, however, yet their marriage couldn't last. They divorced three years later, and he married his secretary and soul mate, Charmian Kittredge. In 1904, Jack became a journalist and reported on the Russo-Japanese War and even covered the Mexican Revolution in 1914.

Wishing to become a prolific writer, Jack set himself to a writing regimen of 1,000 words per day and churned out such classics as his novels *Call of the Wild* (1903), *Sea Wolf* (1904), and *White Fang* (1906) and short story "To Build a Fire" (1910). Soon he became the highest paid and most widely read American author of his time. With his monetary success, Jack built his dream mansion, where he invested most of his money. Before it was finished, he received word that it was burning, and nothing could prevent it from burning to the ground. Down, but not out, Jack continued to write articles, short stories and novels in his little ranch house. He started into ranching that kept his finances from increasing and his need to write to support himself and his wife. Many critics site this as a time where he was turning out quantity rather than quality just to make money. Jack turned to alcohol as an escape from his troubles.

Then, at the age of 40 and suffering from kidney failure, Jack London died of gastro-intestinal uremia on November 22, 1916, a sudden end to the darkening days of Jack's waning life of alcoholism, debt, failing health, and fear of his writing genius extinguishing forever. His works, however, remain as a standing testament to a legacy of literary excellence that few can imitate.

Synopsis

Loretta has just broken up with Billy, a break up that left both heartbroken. The main point of the breakup is that Loretta does not want to marry Billy, though she still harbors feelings for him. Loretta's parents, not liking Billy very much anyway, decide to send Loretta to the Hemingway's. Mrs. Hemingway, upon seeing the young lady, concocts a plan to write to an ex-boyfriend, Ned Bashford, whom she knew before getting married and introduce Loretta to him. Ned is a rather "lazy" Greek who doesn't take women too seriously, and he agrees to visit after reading many of Mrs. Hemingway's letters remarking on Loretta's pure innocence.

Upon meeting Ned, Loretta finds a different kind of man compared to Billy □ a man that cares for her, dotes upon her, and allows her to do things she likes. As Loretta starts to develop more and more of a personality, Ned takes more and more interest in her, seeing her different than other women □ she is honest and real about herself. Then a letter, a letter different from all others, comes from Billy that changes her temperament drastically.

Wishing to find out the cause of her sudden sadness, Ned confronts Loretta, whereupon she confesses to her "wickedness." Ned, not really believing such a woman of virtue could ever be wicked, jokes with her and does not take her words very seriously. She breaks down and tells Ned about Billy and how he wants to marry her. She, of course, doesn't want to marry him, but insists that she must because of her past sin, which gives Ned a rather nasty shock.

Fearing the worst Ned speaks ill of Billy, whom Loretta only defends as being a good man and insists that it is she who is the wicked one and is to blame. Misunderstanding, Ned insists that Loretta must marry Billy for committing this sin. This scares Loretta and she bursts out into tears and confesses her sin...of kissing Billy, such a simple thing.

But what distresses Loretta more is what Billy has told her yesterday □ if a woman kisses a man, she must marry him! And she doesn't want to marry him. Ned then reassures her that she doesn't have to do such a thing and proposes to her...

TEXT

< 1 >

It was because she had broken with Billy that Loretta had come visiting to Santa Clara. Billy could not understand. His sister had reported that he had walked the floor and cried all night. Loretta had not slept all night either, while she had wept most of the night. Daisy knew this, because it was in her arms that the weeping had been done. And Daisy's husband, Captain Kitt, knew, too. The tears of Loretta, and the comforting by Daisy, had lost him some sleep.

Now Captain Kitt did not like to lose sleep. Neither did he want Loretta to marry Billy □ nor anybody else. It was Captain Kitt's belief that Daisy needed the help of her younger sister in the household. But he did not say this aloud. Instead, he always insisted that Loretta was too young to think of marriage. So it was Captain Kitt's idea that Loretta should be packed off on a visit to Mrs. Hemingway. There wouldn't be any Billy there.

Before Loretta had been at Santa Clara a week, she was convinced that Captain Kitt's idea was a good one. In the first place, though Billy wouldn't believe it, she did not want to marry Billy. And in the second place, though Captain Kitt wouldn't believe it, she did not want to leave Daisy. By the time Loretta had been at Santa Clara two weeks, she was absolutely certain that she did not want to marry Billy. But she was not so sure about not wanting to leave Daisy. Not that she loved Daisy less, but that she had doubts.

The day of Loretta's arrival, a nebulous plan began shaping itself in Mrs. Hemingway's brain. The second day she remarked to Jack Hemingway, her husband, that Loretta was so innocent a young thing that were it not for her sweet guilelessness she would be positively stupid. In proof of which, Mrs. Hemingway told her husband several things that made him chuckle. By the third day Mrs. Hemingway's plan had taken recognizable form. Then it was that she composed a letter. On the envelope she wrote: "Mr. Edward Bashford, Athenian Club, San Francisco."

"Dear Ned," the letter began. She had once been violently loved by him for three weeks in her pre-marital days. But she had covenanted herself to Jack Hemingway, who had prior claims, and her heart as well; and Ned Bashford had philosophically not broken his heart over it. He merely added the experience to a large fund of similarly collected data out of which he manufactured philosophy. Artistically and temperamentally he was a Greek □ a tired Greek. He was fond of quoting from Nietzsche, in token that he, too, had passed through the long sickness that follows upon the ardent search for truth; that he too had emerged too experienced, too shrewd, too profound, ever again to be afflicted by the madness of youths in their love of truth. "'To worship appearance,'" he often quoted; "'to believe in forms, in tones, in words, in the whole Olympus of appearance!'" This particular excerpt he always concluded with, "'Those Greeks were superficial □ out of profundity!'"

< 2 >

He was a fairly young Greek, jaded and worn. Women were faithless and unveracious, he held □ at such times that he had relapses and descended to pessimism from his wonted high philosophical calm. He did not believe in the truth of women; but, faithful to his German master, he did not strip from them the airy gauzes that veiled their untruth. He was content to accept them as appearances and to make the best of it. He was superficial □ out of profundity.

"Jack says to be sure to say to you, 'good swimming,' Mrs. Hemingway wrote in her letter, "and also 'to bring your fishing duds along.'" Mrs. Hemingway wrote other things in the letter. She told him that at last she was prepared to exhibit to him an absolutely true, unsullied, and innocent woman. "A more guileless, immaculate bud of womanhood never blushed on the planet," was one of the several ways in which she phrased the inducement. And to her husband she said triumphantly, "If I don't marry Ned off this time □ " leaving unstated the terrible alternative that she lacked either vocabulary to express or imagination to conceive.

Contrary to all her forebodings, Loretta found that she was not unhappy at Santa Clara. True, Billy wrote to her every day, but his letters were less distressing than his presence. Also, the ordeal of being away from Daisy was not so severe as she had expected. For the first time in her life she was not lost in eclipse in the blaze of Daisy's brilliant and mature personality. Under such favorable circumstances Loretta came rapidly to the front, while Mrs.

Hemingway modestly and shamelessly retreated into the background.

Loretta began to discover that she was not a pale orb shining by reflection. Quite unconsciously she became a small centre of things. When she was at the piano, there was some one to turn the pages for her and to express preferences for certain songs. When she dropped her handkerchief, there was some one to pick it up. And there was some one to accompany her in ramblings and flower gatherings. Also, she learned to cast flies in still pools and below savage riffles, and how not to entangle silk lines and gut-leaders with the shrubbery.

Jack Hemingway did not care to teach beginners, and fished much by himself, or not at all, thus giving Ned Bashford ample time in which to consider Loretta as an appearance. As such, she was all that his philosophy demanded. Her blue eyes had the direct gaze of a boy, and out of his profundity he delighted in them and forbore to shudder at the duplicity his philosophy bade him to believe lurked in their depths. She had the grace of a slender flower, the fragility of color and line of fine china, in all of which he pleasured greatly, without thought of the Life Force palpitating beneath and in spite of Bernard Shaw - in whom he believed.

< 3 >

Loretta bourgeoned. She swiftly developed personality. She discovered a will of her own and wishes of her own that were not everlastingly entwined with the will and the wishes of Daisy. She was petted by Jack Hemingway, spoiled by Alice Hemingway, and devotedly attended by Ned Bashford. They encouraged her whims and laughed at her follies, while she developed the pretty little tyrannies that are latent in all pretty and delicate women. Her environment acted as a soporific upon her ancient desire always to live with Daisy. This desire no longer prodded her as in the days of her companionship with Billy. The more she saw of Billy, the more certain she had been that she could not live away from Daisy. The more she saw of Ned Bashford, the more she forgot her pressing need of Daisy.

Ned Bashford likewise did some forgetting. He confused superficiality with profundity, and entangled appearance with reality until he accounted them one. Loretta was different from other women. There was no masquerade about her. She was real. He said as much to Mrs. Hemingway, and more, who agreed with him and at the same time caught her husband's eyelid drooping down for the moment in an unmistakable wink.

It was at this time that Loretta received a letter from Billy that was somewhat different from his others. In the main, like all his letters, it was pathological. It was a long recital of symptoms and sufferings, his nervousness, his sleeplessness, and the state of his heart. Then followed reproaches, such as he had never made before. They were sharp enough to make her weep, and true enough to put tragedy into her face. This tragedy she carried down to the breakfast table. It made Jack and Mrs. Hemingway speculative, and it worried Ned. They glanced to him for explanation, but he shook his head.

"I'll find out tonight," Mrs. Hemingway said to her husband.

But Ned caught Loretta in the afternoon in the big living-room. She tried to turn away. He caught her hands, and she faced him with wet lashes and trembling lips. He looked at her, silently and kindly. The lashes grew wetter.

"There, there, don't cry, little one," he said soothingly.

He put his arm protectingly around her shoulder. And to his shoulder, like a tired child, she turned her face. He thrilled in ways unusual for a Greek who has recovered from the long sickness.

< 4 >

"Oh, Ned," she sobbed on his shoulder, "if you only knew how wicked I am!"

He smiled indulgently, and breathed in a great breath freighted with the fragrance of her hair. He thought of his world-experience of women, and drew another long breath. There seemed to emanate from her the perfect sweetness of a child □ 'the aura of a white soul,' was the way he phrased it to himself..

Then he noticed that her sobs were increasing.

"What's the matter, little one?" he asked pettingly and almost paternally. "Has Jack been bullying you? Or has your dearly beloved sister failed to write?"

She did not answer, and he felt that he really must kiss her hair, that he could not be responsible if the situation continued much longer.

"Tell me," he said gently, "and we'll see what I can do."

"I can't. You will despise me. □ Oh, Ned, I am so ashamed!"

He laughed incredulously, and lightly touched her hair with his lips □ so lightly that she did not know.

"Dear little one, let us forget all about it, whatever it is. I want to tell you how I love □ "

She uttered a sharp cry that was all delight, and then moaned –

"Too late!"

"Too late?" he echoed in surprise.

"Oh, why did I? Why did I?" she was moaning.

He was aware of a swift chill at his heart.

"What?" he asked.

"Oh, I . . . he. . . Billy."

"I am such a wicked woman, Ned. I know you will never speak to me again."

"This - er - this Billy," he began haltingly. "He is your brother?"

"No . . . he . . . I didn't know. I was so young. I could not help it. Oh, I shall go mad! I shall go mad!"

It was then that Loretta felt his shoulder and the encircling arm become limp. He drew away from her gently, and gently he deposited her in a big chair, where she buried her face and sobbed afresh. He twisted his mustache fiercely, then drew up another chair and sat down.

"I □ I do not understand," he said.

"I am so unhappy," she wailed.

"Why unhappy?"

"Because . . . he . . . he wants me to marry him."

< 5 >

His face cleared on the instant, and he placed a hand soothingly on hers.

"That should not make any girl unhappy," he remarked sagely. "Because you don't love him is no reason □ of course, you don't love him?"

Loretta shook her head and shoulders in a vigorous negative.

"What?"

Bashford wanted to make sure.

"No," she asserted explosively. "I don't love Billy! I don't want to love Billy!"

"Because you don't love him," Bashford resumed with confidence, "is no reason that you should be unhappy just because he has proposed to you."

She sobbed again, and from the midst of her sobs she cried.

"That's the trouble. I wish I did love him. Oh, I wish I were dead!"

"Now, my dear child, you are worrying yourself over trifles." His other hand crossed over after its mate and rested on hers. "Women do it every day. Because you have changed your mind or did not know your mind, because you have □ to use an unnecessarily harsh word □ jilted a man □ "

"Jilted!" She had raised her head and was looking at him with tear-dimmed eyes. "Oh, Ned, if that were all!"

"All?" he asked in a hollow voice, while his hands slowly retreated hers. He was about to speak further, then remained silent.

"But I don't want to marry him," Loretta broke forth protestingly.

"Then I shouldn't," he counselled.

"But I ought to marry him."

"Ought to marry him?"

She nodded.

"That is a strong word."

"I know it is," she acquiesced, while she strove to control her trembling lips. Then she spoke more calmly. "I am a wicked woman, a terribly wicked woman. No one knows how wicked I am □ except Billy."

There was a pause. Ned Bashford's face was grave, and he looked queerly at Loretta.

"He - Billy knows?" he asked finally.

A reluctant nod and flaming cheeks was the reply.

He debated with himself for a while, seeming, like a diver, to be preparing himself for the plunge.

"Tell me about it." He spoke very firmly. "You must tell me all of it."

"And will you - ever - forgive me?" she asked in a faint, small voice. He hesitated, drew a long breath, and made the plunge.

"Yes," he said desperately. "I'll forgive you. Go ahead."

< 6 >

"There was no one to tell me," she began. "We were with each other so much. I did not know anything of the world - then."

She paused to meditate. Bashford was biting his lip impatiently.

"If I had only known □ "

She paused again.

"Yes, go on," he urged.

"We were together almost every evening."

"Billy?" he demanded, with a savageness that startled her.

"Yes, of course, Billy. We were with each other so much. . . . . If I had only known. . . . . There was no one to tell me. . . . . I was so young □ "

Her lips parted as though to speak further, and she regarded him anxiously.

"The scoundrel!"

With the explosion Ned Bashford was on his feet, no longer a tired Greek, but a violently angry young man.

"Billy is not a scoundrel; he is a good man," Loretta defended with a firmness that surprised Bashford.

"I suppose you'll be telling me next that it was all your fault," he said sarcastically.

She nodded.

"What?" he shouted.

"It was all my fault," she said steadily. "I should never have let him, I was to blame."

Bashford ceased from his pacing up and down, and when he spoke his voice was resigned.

"All right," he said. "I don't blame you in the least, Loretta. And you have been very honest. But Billy is right, and you are wrong. You must get married."

"To Billy?" she asked, in a dim, far-away voice.

"Yes, to Billy. I'll see to it. Where does he live? I'll make him."

"But I don't want to marry Billy!" she cried out in alarm. "Oh, Ned, you won't do that?"

"I shall," he answered sternly. "You must. And Billy must. Do you understand?"

Loretta buried her face in the cushioned chair back, and broke into a passionate storm of sobs.

All that Bashford could make out at first, as he listened, was: "But I don't want to leave Daisy! I don't want to leave Daisy!"

He paced grimly back and forth, then stopped curiously to listen.

"How was I to know? – Boo-hoo," Loretta was crying. "He didn't tell me. Nobody else ever kissed me. I never dreamed a kiss could be so terrible. . .until, boo-hoo. . .until he wrote to me. I only got the letter this morning."

< 7 >

His face brightened. It seemed as though light was dawning on him.

"Is that what you're crying about?"

"N-no."

His heart sank.

"Then what are you crying about?" he asked in a hopeless voice.

"Because you said I had to marry Billy. And I don't want to marry Billy. I don't want to leave Daisy. I don't know what I want. I want. I wish I were dead."

He nerved himself for another effort.

"Now look here, Loretta, be sensible. What is this about kisses? You haven't told me everything."

"I □ I don't want to tell you everything."

She looked at him beseechingly in the silence that fell. "Must I ?" she quavered finally.

"You must," he said imperatively. "You must tell me everything."

"Well, then . . . must I?"

"You must."

"He. . . I . . . we . . ." she began flounderingly. Then blurted out, "I let him, and he kissed me."

"Go on," Bashford commanded desperately.

"'That's all," she answered.

"All?" There was a vast incredulity in his voice.

"All?" In her voice was an interrogation no less vast.

"I mean - er - nothing worse?" He was overwhelmingly aware of his own awkwardness.

"Worse?" She was frankly puzzled. "As though there could be! Billy said □"

"When did he say it?" Bashford demanded abruptly.

"In his letter I got this morning. Billy said that my . . . our . . . our kisses were terrible if we didn't get married." Bashford's head was swimming.

"What else did Billy say?" he asked.

"He said that when a woman allowed a man to kiss her, she always married him □ that it was terrible if she didn't. It was the custom, he said; and I say it is a bad, wicked custom, and I don't like it. I know I'm terrible," she added defiantly, "but I can't help it."

Bashford absent-mindedly brought out a cigarette.

"Do you mind if I smoke?" he asked, as he struck a

match.

Then he came to himself.

"I beg your pardon," he cried, flinging away match and cigarette. "I don't want to smoke. I didn't mean that at all. What I mean is □"

He bent over Loretta, caught her hands in his, then sat on the arm of the chair and softly put one arm around her.

< 8 >

"Loretta, I am a fool. I mean it. And I mean something more. I want you to be my wife."

He waited anxiously in the pause that followed.

"You might answer me," he urged.

"I will . . . if □"

"Yes, go on. If what?"

"If I don't have to marry Billy."

"You can 't marry both of us," he almost shouted.

"And it isn't the custom . . . what . . . what Billy said?"

"No, it isn't the custom. Now, Loretta, will you marry me?"

"Don't be angry with me," she pouted demurely.

He gathered her into his arms and kissed her.

"I wish it were the custom," she said in a faint voice, from the midst of the embrace, "because then I'd have to marry you, Ned . . . dear. . .wouldn't I?"

EXPLANATION OF
Words & Idioms

Acquiesce: (v) to agree without complaint.
Ample: (adj) a lot of.
Ardent: (adj) using great emotion; passionate.
Assert: (v) to speak in defense.
Beseechingly: (adv) to act in a begging manner.
Burgeon: (v) to grow.
Covenant: (v) to promise.
Dud: (n) clothing.
Duplicity: (n) lie.
Flounderingly: (adv) to speak with uncertainty.
Freight: (v) carry.
Gauze: (n) mist or haze.
Guilelessness: (n) innocent or without cunning.
Gut-leader: (n) a strong, heavy line linking the end of a fishing line to a hook.
Immaculate: (adj) perfect; clean and pure.
Imperatively: (adv) to speak with pleading.
Incredulously: (adv) with disbelief.
Inducement: (n) something said to urge someone into action.
Interrogation: (n) official questioning.
Jaded: (adj) cynical or pessimistic.
Jilted: (adj) to reject the love of or be rejected by a person.
Nebulous: (adj) giant and without form.
Nietzsche: (1844-1900) a German philosopher; argued

against the worldly importance of Christianity.

Palpitate: (v) to move or pump quickly like a heart.

Pathological: (adj) habitual behavior that is also obsessive.

Pettingly: (adv) to speak in a demeaning or debasing manner.

Plunge: (n) a dive or a swim.

Profundity: (n) a great intelligence.

Queerly: (adv) strangely.

Resigned: (adj) accepting.

Riffle: (n) water made shallow by sand or rock.

Shrewd: (adj) to have sharp intelligence.

Soporific: (n) a sleeping drug.

Superficiality: (n) nonsense or shallowness.

Token: (n) evidence or proof.

Unsullied: (adj) pure.

Study Questions

1. What kind of a person is Loretta? What kind of a person is Billy? What kind of a person is Ned? Give good examples to support your answers.

2. Why does kissing Billy distress Loretta so much? Is it because kissing was so shocking back then, or is it because Loretta is so naïve and innocent? Give examples to support your answer.

3. The story ends on a rather open-ended note. "'I wish it were the custom,' she said in a faint voice, from the midst of the embrace, 'because then I'd have to marry you, Ned . . . dear. . .wouldn't I?'" What does this final quote, taken with all that we have read before, actually mean? What character trait is Loretta showing here? Is she really the manipulated simpleton others would believe her to be? Give examples to explain your answer.

4. Is Loretta really a wicked woman? Is Billy wicked? Why or why not?

5. What are the differences between Billy and Ned? Who do you think the better man is? Why?

6. Jack London was a supporter of women's suffrage. Do you see this story as pro-feminist? Why or why not?

VII. FÜR ELISE

by Steven Reeder

Author

Synopsis

Text

Words & Idioms

Study Questions

INTRODUCTION OF THE AUTHOR:
Steven Reeder (Born 1972)

Born on a Southern Alberta cattle ranch west of the Canadian Rockies, Steven lived in the most mundane environment to cultivate his imagination. He would have to sit for most of the day on tractors, farming the rocky soil for alfalfa hay, with nothing to do but think up stories. Without a radio, Steven would often hold his own radio programs, DJ and songs included, screaming out the tunes above the steady roar of the tractor, to whittle the hours away as he circled through the seemingly endless prairie farmland. His father, Bill, is a professional cowboy and tried to rub the western mentality onto his son, but Steven was too much of a dreamer for the serious everyday work of a rancher.

As soon as he graduated high school, Steven packed up and went south to the United States to gain an education as an architect. Realizing he had a hidden love for the arts, he decided to change his major, but not before he decided to go away to Korea for two years as a missionary to study and teach the people in their own tongue; he worked and served in Seoul and the Kang Won Province. He was only nineteen at the time. Upon his return he entered Brigham Young University to study English literature where he became serious about writing short stories and plays. He even won honorable mentions in the *Writer's Digest* playwright competition.

After graduating three years later, he returned to Korea

to teach English. He started off in Suncheon, the South Cholla Province, where he taught at a language institute for a year and then at a private high school for two years. It was there that he met his wife, Jeong Hwa, and was married. They moved to Andong where he started teaching at the national university, and during his two-year stay there, he had his first child, Kaysha. He received his M.A. degree in the Humanities at California State University through correspondence courses. He moved to Busan next and started teaching at Dongseo University, where he has continued teaching up to the present and was blessed with his second child, Christopher Kade.

Steven continues writing; he has written a fantasy novel and is currently working on the second. His love for the fantasy books of J.R.R. Tolkien and Frank Herbert have been the greatest influences in his writing. His short story, "Für Elise" was written during his wife's pregnancy in Andong. He decided to experiment with mixed media by taking Beethoven's classical composition of the same name and Shakespeare's "Sonnet 18" and rework the themes into a short story.

He hopes to continue writing, and after tweaking his novel for the umpteenth time, perhaps he will feel good enough to publish it. Until then, he will see just how this little experiment will go.

Synopsis

The story starts with the first half of Shakespeare's "Sonnet 18" that explains in detail the beauty of a woman. Pieter Bruadel is reading this to his class. Pieter is a rather temperamental English teacher who feels more emotion for his poem than for the students. One student in particular, Sean (pronounced Shawn), is very bored with his poem and lets everyone know it. His tantrums upset Pieter to the point that he sets out to prove through even more words that a poem is an extension of the poet's desire, that a poem offers life to things which are dead. Only one student seems to understand his passion, Sandra, while the rest laugh at Sean's outbursts.

Pieter finally looses control and his composure, going off in a rant about second chances that only alienates his class further. The class bell rings and the students scamper out of class. Pieter goes to his desk in the corner to gain control of his emotions; he cannot get the woman out of his mind. Putting his head on his desk, he thinks of long ago to a time when he was truly young and mortal.

He remembers sitting in a coach escorting a beautiful woman, Elise, to his manor. He remembers being a Duke who commanded respect. He remembers Gabriel. They stop at a river where Elise is to tell Gabriel for the final time that she does not love him and that she chooses Pieter. He remembers Gabriel's feeble attempts to win her love back, but she is too enamored with Pieter. They leave with Gabriel defeated.

Pieter takes her to his castle where they are to

consummate their love through a ritual. He has contacted the most powerful warlock in the land who has the knowledge of eternal life. The potion he has concocted works on the love of the imbiber. If the person truly loves then they shall live as long as that love lasts. If that love is a lie, they will die at that very moment. They are interrupted by Gabriel who has come to convince the Duke that Elise still loves him. The Duke ignores the peasant and returns to his love. Pieter partakes first. Elise partakes next...she gags, chokes, and then dies. Her love was a lie. Not knowing this or exactly what happened, Pieter blames the warlock who explains exactly what has occurred.

Crestfallen, Pieter demands to be alone where he wallows in the sorrow of his love. He will always love her; he is doomed to love her. Thus he will live as long as that love stands. He sits to craft a poem in remembrance of Elise, for as long as he lives, she will live as well in memory and through the words of the poem.

The next period bell drags Pieter from his thoughts of his past only to find Sandra standing before his desk. She seems to understand his pain and voices her thoughts. She then leaves the room and her teacher to his own self pity. He looks down at the last lines of the poem, and knows that Elise has also survived the bands of death through the power of the poem.

TEXT

Shall I compare thee to a summer's day?
Thou art more lovely and more temperate:
Rough winds do shake the darling buds of May,
And summer's lease hath all to short a date:
Sometimes too hot the eye of heaven shines,
And often in his gold complexion dimmed
And every fair from fair sometimes declines,
By chance or nature's changing course untrimmed...

"Yahhhh!" A yawn of boredom broke the silent air of Mr. Braudel's temperamental recital of the Elizabethan sonnet. Pieter Braudel peered up from the text, and his owlish eyes shot a hurtful glance toward Sean Casey who stretched the boredom out, hands grasping for the ceiling.

"Something bores you, Sean?" he asked with an icy air.

"Man, I can't take any more of this stuff! It's boring me to death."

Mr. Braudel's delicate eyebrows shot up in surprise. He could not believe the boy's lack of emotion. He shook his head, his frazzled, caramel hair whipping back and forth in an almost comical fashion as he approached Sean. The boy didn't even bat an eye, obviously not concerned with Mr. Braudel's excessive emotion, as if it were nothing new.

"Do you realize the power a poem truly holds, Sean?" Mr. Braudel asked, his voice full of sorrow.

Sean just wrinkled his nose with contempt and guffawed. "The only power a poem can hold is that it puts me to sleep."

All the blood drained from Pieter's face. His breathing grew heavier, but he sniffed back his anger. *Why doesn't he realize?* Sean's lack of concern cut deep into his soul.

"That's because you don't know the power of a poem. It offers life to that which is dead." Pieter's voice cracked on the last word and many of the students suppressed snickers. All became sober again under their teacher's baleful eye. He clutched at his composure and continued with a more stoic tone, "It's the voice of a poet reaching out for that which he loves."

Shaking his head with a muffled laugh Sean replied, "Yeah, a bunch of pompous windbags sitting around writing of women they only wish they could have. I'll show you how men get women." The class busted out in laughter, and Mr. Braudel's flared his nostrils in controlled rage as Sean ran his fingers across Sandra's smooth nape. The boy had no respect for anyone, not even the girl sitting in front of him □ the only student, it seemed, who took the class seriously; Mr. Braudel's prized student. She turned with an icy glare.

"You don't know what women want!" she snapped.

"Oh yeah?" Sean said, winking and flapping his tongue at her. "They want a real man." She whirled back around with disgust, her long auburn hair brushing at his offensive gestures.

"Sean!" Braudel raised his voice, breaking the tension. He would not sit and watch him badger the girl. "That will be enough out of you. No more you hear?" Sean nodded his head in mechanical agreement. With a deep breath,

Braudel tried to salvage the class. "Now, from what we have read so far, what do you think the poem is saying, Sean?"

Looking down at his paper, he ignorantly replied, "I . . . I don't know, man; a guy in tights drooling over some pale babe showing lots of cleavage?" Again more laughter from his peers resounded of the cold brick walls

"Class!" All went silent under his vindictive eye. "This is not some frivolous play, but a poem of a fair maiden's beauty. The poet wants to express the beauty and characteristics of his only love. Don't you feel it?" *He doesn't know.* After tapping the book, he continued, "This is true love."

"I'll bet!" Sean interrupted once again. "Sounds like some loner trying to sway his chick in the sack." Another roar of laughter burst out uncontrollably from his class mates.

Pieter couldn't contain himself any longer. *Elise! Oh God no, Elise!* He was too flustered.

"How can you be so damn flippant and uncaring of other's feelings?" he snapped bitterly. "Can't you feel the pain of the poet? His yearning for his lost love? My God, Sean!" His voice became high and hysterical with grief. *My Love, what is it?!* "Have you never loved? What is there left of us if we cannot love? I . . . I . . . sit here every day and wonder what it would be like if I hadn't been so quick to judge. Where would my life be now if I chose differently? That thought goes through my head every single second of every single miserable day!"

He could see the class shift uncomfortably and shoot quick glances with each other, but enough was enough. They had to know! They had to know the true meaning of the poem.

Pieter continued with painful fervor. *What have you done?!* "I wonder what I have been reduced to. I wanted to bring her passion for all the world to see. I hoped to plant it in the hearts of the youth, but you don't seem to care! No one cares! No one cares about the dead anymore. What is dead is dead! You all live for the now, but what of the past?! What honor will you bring for the past? Huh? . . . What?! No derivative remarks, Sean?" Pieter's sorrow-etched eyes sized up Sean's indifferent form.

Silence. A lone fluorescent light flickered periodically above, creating an incessant buzz that only added to the sharpness of the silence.

The period bell rang, cracking the quiet air with a piercing shriek. The whole classroom disrupted into a hysteric mass of slamming books and senseless conversation as the room cleared out at a maddened pace. Pieter still stood wantonly, craning over the desk where Sean had sat. His trembling form locked into that position, a statue. Then slowly, reason fluttered into his scrambling brain and all the tense muscles in Pieter's body relaxed as he sagged like a marionette hanging on a peg. A Tear began to trickle down his cheek. *Why doesn't anybody care?* The dismayed Pieter Braudel loafed over to his desk in the corner of the room; with a swollen heart, he sank into his padded chair. "*Pieter waits for me.*" Following the blessed silence, he dropped his face into his cupped hands and wept.

"Mr. Braudel?" A nervous, cracking voice broke through the stillness.

Pieter looked up out of his hands, his eyes bloodshot and ashamed. He tried to force a smile at Sandra standing in front of his desk, kicking her feet with uncomfortable nervousness.

"Is everything okay?" she asked innocently. "I mean, I know you've always held compassion for your poetry; but today, I think you scared the whole class." She tried to add a chuckle, but he knew it was out nerves. She was afraid for him, maybe a little concerned. He closed his eyes in shame.

"It seems like so long ago," Pieter finally spoke, barely audible. "I don't know why I still feel so strongly." He locked his gaze back on hers, his chin trembling. "It was so long ago."

Sandra shuffled under the uncomfortable stare. "I think I should be getting to my next class." She turned without further comment and more than quickly walked out of the classroom. Pieter's tear stung eyes followed her out before he gazed down at the book on his desk. The phantom voice of the past returned. "*I think it's true love this time.*"

"It was so long ago," he sighed.

Gazing down at the poem, he breathed out with anguish, "Oh, Elise. How could I have been so foolish? The pain I carry now was nothing I could ever have comprehended." Nestling his tear streaked face in the fold of his arm, the young English teacher slipped into a gentle sleep. Dreams of his long lost love's delicate back walking toward the river clouded his memory.

"Elise! Elise! Over here!" A bright eyed, buoyant young man had motioned the petite woman toward the swollen river away from the carriage, but not too far away. "How was your holiday?"

"Uh, it could have been better. Daddy was a blubbering drunk the whole two weeks."

Pieter stepped out of the carriage on the opposite side of the conversing couple, watching them warily. His lissom body seemed to glide through the trees, walking stick in hand, as his sharp eyes penetrated the young man talking to Elise.

"The ride was safe, I presume?" the young man had the nerve to ask, as if she were traveling with some sort of brute and not a gentleman.

"Oh, yes. The driver was most kind, although the coach was a bit uncomfortable. But I survived." A cheerful grin swept across her cherry lips. Pieter scowled from his position in the trees. *She has to always be the flirt.*

The young man grinned, captivated by her light green eyes. A grin that sucked in the sunshine, her beauty, everything and then offered it back as if gift. "You know, you are even more beautiful than when you left."

"Oh, Gabe!" Elise turned in embarrassment, her face blushing, "Please don't start. You know it makes me feel uncomfortable."

"You really didn't mind before. Come on. Let's go on a romantic stroll down the river." As he reached for her white-gloved hand, Pieter had to put a stop to it. The woman was still weak.

"Elise darling! Aren't you coming dear? We'll be late," he

yelled, threading his way through the trees back to the carriage with a suppressed grin. The woman would come. She always followed the real money.

Elise turned to the shocked Gabriel, "I'm sorry Gabe. The reason why I came here was to tell you good-bye." Her lily-white skin flushed with color. She affected a coquettish smile.

"Good-bye? After all we've been through? What we've had?" Gabriel's leathery face paled. His beaming grin had faded to a limp pout.

A smile cracked on Pieter's face as he continued to peer from behind the carriage.

"All friends must go on Gabe," Elise said.

"Friends? That's all we've been to each other is friends?"

"That's all it was meant to be."

Shaking his head in bewilderment, he refused, "No. It's been more than that. You can't betray our love like this."

Elise faltered, losing her cool composure. "Our love? No, my dear friend, it's always been your love. We've known each other since youth." Then brushing off her dress as she wrestled the calm out of her bosom she added, "You are like my brother." Then she giggled. "Anything more than that is simply preposterous."

Dipping down on one knee, he grasped Elise's hand looking into her eyes, "Then marry me. Leave with me right now. I will be at your will. Then will you truly know of my love."

Giggling again, she purred, "You could always make me laugh, Gabe." Running her hand through his flaxen hair, she continued, "But I must go on."

Tears streaked down Gabriel's cheeks.

"Pieter waits for me," she continued. "He's in an awful hurry. I must go." She bent down and brushed a kiss past his cheek. "I think it's true love this time," she said, then turned and ran for the black coach. Pieter stood at the open door and escorted her into the seat as he mustered all his power to ignore the paramour at the river's edge. When the coach departed, she poked her head out for a final farewell, "Keep in touch Gabe," she said. "We will always be friends."

At the edge of the villa Shalmar, a rustic citadel sat alone above the lush land with its towers nestled gently in a crown of clouds. Inside the rough, bleak walls of the cold stone castle flowered the warm love of Duke Pieter of Wheinsmark as he reclined with his fresh love in his arms. In the den, the two lovers embraced, captured by each other's beauty.

"You know the power that love holds?" Pieter said, breaking the immaculate silence.

"I've never really thought about it."

"It's eternal."

"Don't be silly, Love. Nothing lasts forever."

"Yes. But love is the only thing that can last through time."

"But what of death?"

"Death is an obstacle that love overcomes."

Silence followed as the lovers kissed, a Judas kiss as he reflected on it now. The cracking embers of the soft glowing fire only added to the ecstasy. Pieter gazed down on Elise's long cinnamon hair flowing down her ivory face in ringlets coming to rest on her breasts. *I'm the luckiest man alive. Wealthy beyond my dreams with a lady more beautiful than any heaven could create.* He smiled and kissed her smooth forehead, capturing a giggle from his rapt lover.

"When we marry it shall be as eternal as our love," he said breaking the quiet again as he stared into his sweet love's eyes that sparkled like the clearest lagoon on a bright afternoon.

"I've never heard of anything so foolish."

"It's wonderful," Pieter said with a provocative smile. "Through the power of love, our marriage is forever sealed and will carry us throughout eternity."

"And wealth and fame will accompany us? We will still have all the popularity, won't we? Oh, I do wish to be married as soon as possible."

"Yes. For this is life eternal. What we have now will increase ten fold in eternity."

Elise could only smile at such a prospect.

"My Liege," a rough voice in the shadows shattered the unity of the lovers like a cold chisel harshly dividing solid stone asunder. "I have come according to your summons."

"Ah, Antorax. Come, sit down." Pieter rose to meet his guest. "I would like you to meet my fiancée. We are to be married tomorrow."

Bowing, the dark cloaked man sat down before Elise, stating his pleasantries. Out of courtesy, he folded the hood of his cloak back over his head and around his neck, pulling his pasty face from its shadows to look the fair maiden straight in the eyes. An extremely cadaverous but wizened face with glazed eyes latched onto hers, stagnated as if judging her. Pieter didn't like that kind of look.

"You requested the elixir of eternal life, Sire?" his throaty voice cracked as he turned his attention to the Duke.

"Yes, friend Antorax." Pieter replied, "We don't wish to live a life together only to be separated at death."

"You ask for that which is impossible, Sire. It requires true love to endure the bands of time."

"So be it." Pieter pulled Elise closer to him, "Our love will conquer the insurmountable odds to gain immortality."

The cloaked figure procured a crystal vial from the folds of his black robe, "This is the power of the eternities, the elixir of eternal life. Be forewarned, it is not a power to be trifled with, for it is only true love that separates the mundane from the divine."

"Well spoken, Antorax!" Pieter said. "Let the gods tremble at the power of our love."

Antorax relinquished the vial over to the young Duke as Elise griped his hand in anticipation, her smile growing wider by the second. With excitement sparkling in her iridescent eyes, she reached over and grabbed the vial. Power surged through the lovers' hands. Pieter watched Elise close her eyes in ecstasy; his heart picked up the pace. The power flowing from the vial was strong. Pieter wondered at the effect it would hold on them in their system. The moment was rapturous.

"Master!" the steward's voice broke the lovers' trance and forced Antorax to slither back into the shadows. Seeing the Duke's poisonous glower, the steward gulped down his fear and kept his form. "There is a stranger from afar with urgent business."

"Why do you disturb me?" Pieter barked. "Do you not value your life? I told you not to disturb me at this hour!"

"S . . . s . . . sorry, Master, but the foreigner says your life is in danger," the steward said overcoming his fear.

"Thank-you. You may leave." Turning back to Elise with a fatigued sigh, "I'll be back, Love. Don't move." He leaned over, pressed his lips to her forehead, and forced himself to the entrance.

At the bottom of the marble stairs, Pieter glanced upon his guest, an average looking fellow wearing below the average clothes. *No friend of mine.* The stranger, upon meeting the Duke, bowed before him.

"Gabriel of Antioch, at your service."

"What is your business, commoner?" Pieter regarded the man with disdain.

"You may not know me, but we briefly met . . . at the river."

Narrowing his eyes in thought, Pieter nodded his head upon recognition, "Ah, yes. Elise's school chum. How charming to meet you. You know we are to be married?"

"Yes. That's why I've come."

"If you think to stop this marriage, remember I have power in this land."

"I know."

"Well then, out with it!"

"I've come to warn you."

"Warn me?" Pieter laughed. "What could you possibly warn me about, peasant?"

"Elise doesn't love you," Gabriel said with an air of

indifference.

Pieter bellowed out in laughter, "You know not of our love."

"But I know her."

"You knew her!" Pieter burst out, his smile barreled over by his impatient sneer.

"If you marry her, you'll be the fool everyone takes you for."

The Duke lashed out his right hand, catching the unsuspected commoner on the chin. "She loves me. Something you will never feel, peasant!"

Gabriel rubbed his chin and grinned at the Duke, the same grin that threatened all the Duke cared for. "She doesn't love you."

"What makes you think that?"

"Because she still loves me."

Pieter's lip curled in disgust. He could not believe the nerve of this commoner coming before him to dictate the affairs of his life.

"If she still loves you then why is she in my bed chamber as we speak? You could never fulfill her needs, not like I can. People change, so just accept your loss and be on your way." Pieter brushed his hands at Gabriel, an exclamation of the finality of his statement. Gabriel either chose to ignore the arrogant gesture or was ignorant of it, for he kept on speaking.

"She went to you to make me jealous. I have known her since youth, and I have never tried to win her. You may have won her at Antioch, in front of her father, but I will win her back!" Gabriel pulled his glove off with an arrogance not seen in a commoner before nobility and threw it down at the Dukes feet.

"I could have you contained in chains," Pieter said venomously.

"But you would not have won Elise's love. Throw down your gauntlet. The last man standing deserves Elise's love. Fate will decide who deserves Elise more. Fate never lies."

Pieter's grim features lightened as he tried to suppress his laughter. Gabriel gawked in unbelief. He stood his ground, face reddening with anger, "She still loves me! Throw down your gauntlet!"

Pieter laughed in his face.

"Peasants truly are amusing," he said wiping the tears from his eyes. With that Pieter turned and lumbered up the stairs, bursting out into another fit of laughter. He turned to see Gabriel standing as stone in shock, face blood red. Feeling the fool, Gabriel picked up his glove and glanced up at the Duke, then turned and stormed out of the chamber as Pieter broke out into another fit of mocking laughter.

Within the den, Elise was stretched out on the chesterfield, talking lightly with Antorax. She acknowledged Pieter's presence with joy in her eyes.

"Who was that?" she gaily asked.

"Just an annoying peddler," he said wiping the remains of moisture from his eyes. "His commonality caught me off guard. I've sent the dogs after him for the servants' amusement. He won't bother us again." Tucking in his formal composure, he moved over and knelt before her. "Now, are you ready?"

"Yes. I can feel it."

"Good." He said, uncapping the vial, hands shaking in

anticipation, "I will partake first."

"Remember," Antorax broke in, "The eternities come only from the love you hold for the other. There is nothing more powerful than true love."

Pieter swallowed half the vial holding his love's gaze in his. Finishing, he proffered it to her.

"I love you," he said plainly.

She just smiled in return.

Putting the crystal vial to her lush, cherry lips, Pieter squeezed her hand as she swallowed.

"Now this is love eternal," he said as they embraced each other and kissed passionately, deeply. Pieter never felt such rapture, such love. His bosom was filled with an overwhelming joy. *So this is godhood. A coupling of love so overwhelming not even death can destroy it* .

Elise suddenly clutched his hand in a deathly grip as she chocked, gasping for air like a beached fish. His revere melted into horror as he watched Elise's beautiful features twist and contort into shudders of pain.

"My love, what is it?!" Pieter wailed out.

"My . . . my chest . . . can't . . . breath!" Elise's velvety voice distorted into guttural hacks sputtering from her twisting lips. Her pristine face became sallow with revolt.

Her grip became weaker and weaker as painful convulsions slowly shook her life away. Grabbing her, Pieter cried out, "Elise! Oh God no, Elise!" Shooting a glance toward the cloaked figure, spat out, "What have you done?! What have you done, you Warlock?! What have you done to my love?" Tears streamed down his eyes.

"It is not what I have done, but what she has done," the

wizened old man said, bowing his head.

Pieter looked back at his now lifeless maiden, her features paling with death. With sobs of sorrow, he gave a final kiss to his sweet Elise. Gently he pushed her eyelids closed with his trembling hand, forever sealing her green eyes in darkness. For minutes that seemed like hours, he couldn't move from Elise's breast. Sobs wracked his body.

"Our love is eternal," he growled at her chest. "You partook of the power of love. We are immortal."

"Death is the obstacle love overcomes," the warlock broke in.

"Yes, I remember," Pieter whispered to himself, suppressing his rage.

"She is dead, but your love is still eternal."

"Must I be damned by such foolish love?" Grabbing his composure, the Duke rose from the floor and sighed out a last bit of grief. "Leave! I must be alone."

"As you wish, Sire," Antorax bowed and disappeared into the shadows without a sound.

Warily glancing through the sputtering shadow, Pieter sat himself before the fire, satisfied that he was now alone. Pieter stared blankly at his mortal love. *The body dies. The portrait fades away. A sculpture erodes to nothingness. But words stand the test of time, and they bring to life that which is dead.*

"But as long as I live, so shall you," he brushed his hand past her pale cheek. With new resolve, he wiped the tears from his cheeks and picked up a quill from the side table. The feather quill scratched through the silence on the parchment as Pieter immortalized his dear love in ageless words, sealed by tears of his eternal love.

Pieter had awoken to the sound of the period bell ringing. He snapped his head up at the figure standing at the doorway. It was Sandra.

"I'm sure she was pretty," she said with childlike innocence. "I . . . I overheard you talking in your sleep. I'm sorry she died. She must have loved you."

"*I think it's true love this time.*"

She then turned and walked out of the room.

Pieter's heart burned. He truly longed for Elise's love as his love still groped out for her through the ages. He shook his head with disgust; he was only living in arrogance. But no matter the pain, he would always love her, could do nothing but love her; for that is all he had left. Sucking in a deep breath he looked down at his poem, and through tear streaked eyes, he knew Elise would never die.

...But thy eternal summer shall not fade,
Nor loose possession of that fair thou ow'st;
Nor shall death brag thou wander'st in his shade:
When in eternal lines to time thou grow'st:
So long as men can breathe, or eyes can see,
So long lives this, and this gives life to thee.

William Shakespeare

EXPLANATION OF
Words & Idioms

Affect: (v) to act on the emotion of.
Art: (v) are; now archaic.
Badger: (v) to annoy or harass.
Baleful: (adj) threatening.
Bat an eye: (expression) blink or express an emotion.
Brute: (n) a person lacking manners.
Buoyant: (adj) cheerful or optimistic.
Cadaverous: (adj) looking like a corpse.
Chick: (slang) a young woman.
Coquettish: (adj) flirtatious.
Eye of heaven: (expression) the sun.
Falter: (v) to speak with hesitations, to stammer
Flaxen: (adj) a grayish yellow color; blond.
Flippant: (adj) disrespectful.
Fluster: (adj) to be in a state of troubled confusion.
Für: (German) for; Für Elise is the title of one of Beethoven's memorable compositions meaning For Elise.
Gawk: (v) to stare at stupidly.
Glower: (v) to stare at angrily.
Guffaw: (v) to laugh rudely.
Hath: (v) have; now archaic.
Immaculate: (adj) pure.
Incessant: (adj) continuing without interruption.
Iridescent: (adj) appearing multi-colored.
Loaf: (v) to walk absentmindedly.

Lissome: (adj) elegantly slim.

Marionette: (v) a puppet moved by strings from above.

Ow'st: to be indebted to; archaic form of Owe. To decrease the syllable of a word by one, a poet will often remove a vowel to tighten up the stanza (owest=ow'st).

Paramour: (n) a lover, often an adulterous one.

Pompous: (adj) pretentious; especially when using high-sounding words or phrases.

Procure: (v) to get or obtain.

Provocative: (adj) stimulating discussion or exciting controversy.

Rapt: (adj) moved deeply or charmed.

Sputter: (v) to spit out words in an excited manner.

Thee: (pron) rare form of "you" as the object case of "thou"

Thou: (pron) rare form of "you" as the subject case or as the person being addressed.

Wantonly: (adv) without considering the consequences; recklessly.

Warlock: (n) a male witch. Here it is used derogatively for the formal tile of wizard.

Windbag: (slang) a talkative person that says nothing of interest.

Study Questions

1. How does the title play into the story? Does knowing the music help with the tone of the story? Why or why not?

2. What kind of a person is Pieter Braudel? Was he naïve to love such a woman or just a romantic? Explain your answer.

3. Compare and contrast Gabriel with Pieter. Which person is nobler? Were they both foolish in their actions?

4. What kind of a person is Elise? Is it fair that she died? Why or why not?

5. How does the juxtaposition of two different times play into the story? Is it effective or distracting? Explain your answer.

6. Is the story a good interpretation of the Shakespearean sonnet? Why or why not?

7. What purpose do the scattered italicized comments play in the modern setting (i.e. His voice became high and hysterical with grief. "*My Love, what is it?!* Have you never loved?")? Do they in anyway set up the drama that is to come?

8. Though the story is an "alternate universe" setting with magic and wizards, does it still have a sense of believability to it? Why or why not?

VIII. THE IDIOTS

by Joseph Conrad

Author

Synopsis

Text

Words & Idioms

Study Questions

INTRODUCTION OF THE AUTHOR:
Joseph Conrad (1857-1924)

Joseph Conrad was born Józef Teodor Konrad Korzeniowski in Berdichev, Polish Ukraine, a rich area of land that sat between Poland and Russia, on December 3, 1857. Though he was Polish, he would Anglicize his name and write in English to become one of the predecessors of literary modernism. As a boy, Joseph's father was a translator of English and French literature, which gave Joseph a constant exposure to the classics of his time. His grandfather was a captain in the Polish insurrection against Russian annexation, only to loose his land and estate after his country was partitioned between Russia, Austria-Hungary and Prussia. Both his parents, especially his father, were stout Polish patriots, which didn't sit well with Russian authorities of the time. His father moved to Warsaw when Joseph was four to start subversive activities against the Russian presence in Poland. Both his father and mother were arrested and sent to Siberian prison camps where they died of tuberculosis. Joseph lived with his grandmother while his parents suffered in prison, and after their deaths he moved to Switzerland to live with his Uncle, who became his guardian.

With dreams of being a sailor, Joseph joined the French merchant marines in 1870. He eventually joined the British merchant navy where he excelled to the point where he was granted British citizenship and appointed command of his own ship in 1886. It was while in England that he officially anglicized his name to Joseph Conrad. By 1889, Joseph had started his first big steps into becoming a professional writer with the publication of his first novel, *Almayer's Folly*. Though English was his third language, it was the language he chose to write in, based largely on his commitment to England. Joseph's many voyages became the catalyst for many of his works of fiction. His most famous work, *Heart of Darkness* (1899), was inspired by his trip up the African Congo River in 1890.

After the death of his Uncle, he started to date a lady his Uncle had forbidden him to see, Marguerite, on a regular basis, but the difference in their age made it difficult for Joseph to continue seeing her. By 1894, he had retired from seamanship and focused all his attention on writing. He met a lovely woman, Jessie George, an English woman 13 years his junior, and married her in March of 1896. In fact, he wrote his first short story, "The Idiots," during their honeymoon. Though he wrote 19 novels and 21 short stories, Joseph spent his days struggling through his writing, due to the fact that English was his third language, and often failed to notice his wife's pregnancies. Not until 1914, did Joseph see literary success. Before this time, he was often in debt and living off of advances for his writings. He finally reached financial security after the publication of *Chance* in 1914. He was offered knighthood in 1924, which he refused.

Conrad's health was never the best since his youth where he was troubled with rheumatism. When he traveled to America in 1924, he was finally overcome by a heart attack on August 3, which killed him. Though later critics have argued that his language and tone are inexcusably racist, the impact that his writing has left on 20th century English literature cannot be denied, with writers such as T.S. Eliot, Virginia Woolf, Thomas Mann, Ernest Hemingway, F. Scott Fitzgerald, and William Faulkner claiming influence in their writing.

Synopsis

A man narrates of his trip from Treguier to Kervanda and of his first learning of the "idiots," four children □ brothers and sisters □ born to the misfortune of being mentally handicapped. During his trips he learns the tale of their birth, the loss of their parents, and how they came to frequent the road in France he travels upon.

Before the birth of the children, their father, Jean-Pierre Bacadou, had taken over the farm from his father and set out to make it "beloved and fruitful." He marries a beautiful woman, Susan, who pleases his parents and gives birth to twin boys. Their birth is of great satisfaction to Jean-Pierre that he anticipates their coming of age and "wringing tribute from the land." Such joy is not meant to last, for the twins don't grow like the other children and are soon mourned as mentally handicapped by their parents. Jean-Pierre and his wife take the misfortune in stride and try for other children who would grow strong and help in farming the land. With the birth of their third boy, all hope is restored, yet in time this one shows even more slowness than the others.

Susan's mother, Madame Levaille, a rich proprietor of quarries and a pub to service the workers of her quarries, moves in with the struggling couple. Jean-Pierre works himself to the bone, without hope of ever being relieved of the arduous task of farming, and news of a daughter sends him deeper into despair. She, too, soon becomes mentally handicapped.

Jean-Pierre, already an atheist, turns to blaming God as the cause of his woes and swears he will whip any man of the cloth that sets foot upon his land. He sets to drinking and drunken revelry to chase away his misery. He often takes Susan to town to go drinking as well. On the way home one night, he stops at a church and starts cursing God for their lot in life. When Susan tries to say something, he strikes her and knocks her into the back of the wagon. It is abuse she won't put up with for long.

On another night, Susan enters her mother's pub muddy and in disarray. After dismissing the patrons, Madame Levaille discovers her daughter has murdered Jean-Pierre. In a fit of rage, Madame Levaille speaks of her shame and preference of having "idiots" over her own daughter any day. Susan runs out into the night in a crazed manner, scaring many of the seaweed gatherers thinking her a ghost. One worker chases after her, knowing the shadows behind the scream to be only a woman. As he calls out in the darkness, Susan thinks him the wraith of her dead husband, sending her into a maddened frenzy until she runs off a cliff and plummets to her death. The four mentally handicap children are left alone to be tended by Madame Levaille, and wander aimlessly along the road from Treguier to Kervanda during the day, becoming the talk and curiosity of the area.

TEXT

We were driving along the road from Treguier to Kervanda. We passed at a smart trot between the hedges topping an earth wall on each side of the road; then at the foot of the steep ascent before Ploumar the horse dropped into a walk, and the driver jumped down heavily from the box. He flicked his whip and climbed the incline, stepping clumsily uphill by the side of the carriage, one hand on the footboard, his eyes on the ground. After a while he lifted his head, pointed up the road with the end of the whip, and said □

"The idiot!"

The sun was shining violently upon the undulating surface of the land. The rises were topped by clumps of meagre trees, with their branches showing high on the sky as if they had been perched upon stilts. The small fields, cut up by hedges and stone walls that zig-zagged over the slopes, lay in rectangular patches of vivid greens and yellows, resembling the unskilful daubs of a naive picture. And the landscape was divided in two by the white streak of a road stretching in long loops far away, like a river of dust crawling out of the hills on its way to the sea.

"Here he is," said the driver, again.

In the long grass bordering the road a face glided past the carriage at the level of the wheels as we drove slowly by. The imbecile face was red, and the bullet head with close-cropped hair seemed to lie alone, its chin in the dust. The body was lost in the bushes growing thick along the bottom of the deep ditch.

It was a boy's face. He might have been sixteen, judging from the size □ perhaps less, perhaps more. Such creatures are forgotten by time, and live untouched by years till death gathers them up into its compassionate bosom; the faithful death that never forgets in the press of work the most insignificant of its children.

"Ah! There's another," said the man, with a certain satisfaction in his tone, as if he had caught sight of something expected.

There was another. That one stood nearly in the middle of the road in the blaze of sunshine at the end of his own short shadow. And he stood with hands pushed into the opposite sleeves of his long coat, his head sunk between the shoulders, all hunched up in the flood of heat. From a distance he had the aspect of one suffering from intense cold.

"Those are twins," explained the driver.

The idiot shuffled two paces out of the way and looked at us over his shoulder when we brushed past him. The glance was unseeing and staring, a fascinated glance; but he did not turn to look after us. Probably the image passed before the eyes without leaving any trace on the misshapen brain of the creature. When we had topped the ascent I looked over the hood. He stood in the road just where we had left him.

The driver clambered into his seat, clicked his tongue, and we went downhill. The brake squeaked horribly from time to time. At the foot he eased off the noisy mechanism and said, turning half round on his box □

"We shall see some more of them by-and-by."

"More idiots? How many of them are there, then?" I asked.

"There's four of them □ children of a farmer near Ploumar here. . . . The parents are dead now," he added, after a while. "The grandmother lives on the farm. In the daytime they knock about on this road, and they come home at dusk along with the cattle. . . . It's a good farm."

We saw the other two: a boy and a girl, as the driver said. They were dressed exactly alike, in shapeless garments with petticoat-like skirts. The imperfect thing that lived within them moved those beings to howl at us from the top of the bank, where they sprawled amongst the tough stalks of furze. Their cropped black heads stuck out from the bright yellow wall of countless small blossoms. The faces were purple with the strain of yelling; the voices sounded blank and cracked like a mechanical imitation of old people's voices; and suddenly ceased when we turned into a lane.

I saw them many times in my wandering about the country. They lived on that road, drifting along its length here and there, according to the inexplicable impulses of their monstrous darkness. They were an offence to the sunshine, a reproach to empty heaven, a blight on the concentrated and purposeful vigour of the wild landscape. In time the story of their parents shaped itself before me out of the listless answers to my questions, out of the indifferent words heard in wayside inns or on the very road those idiots haunted. Some of it was told by an emaciated and sceptical old fellow with a tremendous whip, while we trudged together over the sands by the side of a two-wheeled cart loaded with dripping seaweed. Then at other times other people confirmed and completed the story: till it stood at last before me, a tale formidable and simple, as they always are, those disclosures of obscure trials endured by ignorant hearts.

When he returned from his military service Jean-Pierre Bacadou found the old people very much aged. He remarked with pain that the work of the farm was not satisfactorily done. The father had not the energy of old days. The hands did not feel over them the eye of the master. Jean-Pierre noted with sorrow that the heap of manure in the courtyard before the only entrance to the house was not so large as it should have been. The fences were out of repair, and the cattle suffered from neglect. At home the mother was practically bedridden, and the girls chattered loudly in the big kitchen, unrebuked, from morning to night. He said to himself: "We must change all this." He talked the matter over with his father one evening when the rays of the setting sun entering the yard between the outhouses ruled the heavy shadows with luminous streaks. Over the manure heap floated a mist, opal-tinted and odorous, and the marauding hens would stop in their scratching to examine with a sudden glance of their round eye the two men, both lean and tall, talking in hoarse tones. The old man, all twisted with rheumatism and bowed with years of work, the younger bony and straight, spoke without gestures in the indifferent manner of peasants, grave and slow. But before the sun had set the father had submitted to the sensible arguments of the son. "It is not for me that I am speaking," insisted Jean-Pierre. "It is for the land. It's a pity to see it badly used. I am not impatient for myself." The old fellow nodded over his stick. "I dare say; I dare say," he muttered. "You may be right. Do what you like. It's the mother that will be pleased."

The mother was pleased with her daughter-in-law. Jean-Pierre brought the two-wheeled spring-cart with a rush into the yard. The gray horse galloped clumsily, and the bride and bridegroom, sitting side by side, were jerked backwards and forwards by the up and down motion of the shafts, in a manner regular and brusque. On the road the distanced wedding guests straggled in pairs and groups. The men advanced with heavy steps, swinging their idle arms. They were clad in town clothes; jackets cut with clumsy smartness, hard black hats, immense boots, polished highly. Their women all in simple black, with white caps and shawls of faded tints folded triangularly on the back, strolled lightly by their side. In front the violin sang a strident tune, and the biniou snored and hummed, while the player capered solemnly, lifting high his heavy clogs. The sombre procession drifted in and out of the narrow lanes, through sunshine and through shade, between fields and hedgerows, scaring the little birds that darted away in troops right and left. In the yard of Bacadou's farm the dark ribbon wound itself up into a mass of men and women pushing at the door with cries and greetings. The wedding dinner was remembered for months. It was a splendid feast in the orchard. Farmers of considerable means and excellent repute were to be found sleeping in ditches, all along the road to Treguier, even as late as the afternoon of the next day. All the countryside participated in the happiness of Jean-Pierre. He remained sober, and, together with his quiet wife, kept out of the way, letting father and mother reap their due of honour and thanks. But the next day he took hold strongly, and the old folks felt a shadow □ precursor of the grave □ fall upon them finally. The world is to the young.

When the twins were born there was plenty of room in the house, for the mother of Jean-Pierre had gone away to dwell under a heavy stone in the cemetery of Ploumar. On that day, for the first time since his son's marriage, the elder Bacadou, neglected by the cackling lot of strange women who thronged the kitchen, left in the morning his seat under the mantel of the fireplace, and went into the empty cow-house, shaking his white locks dismally. Grandsons were all very well, but he wanted his soup at midday. When shown the babies, he stared at them with a fixed gaze, and muttered something like: "It's too much." Whether he meant too much happiness, or simply commented upon the number of his descendants, it is impossible to say. He looked offended □ as far as his old wooden face could express anything; and for days afterwards could be seen, almost any time of the day, sitting at the gate, with his nose over his knees, a pipe between his gums, and gathered up into a kind of raging concentrated sulkiness. Once he spoke to his son, alluding to the newcomers with a groan: "They will quarrel over the land." "Don't bother about that, father," answered Jean-Pierre, stolidly, and passed, bent double, towing a recalcitrant cow over his shoulder.

He was happy, and so was Susan, his wife. It was not an

ethereal joy welcoming new souls to struggle, perchance to victory. In fourteen years both boys would be a help; and, later on, Jean-Pierre pictured two big sons striding over the land from patch to patch, wringing tribute from the earth beloved and fruitful. Susan was happy too, for she did not want to be spoken of as the unfortunate woman, and now she had children no one could call her that. Both herself and her husband had seen something of the larger world □ he during the time of his service; while she had spent a year or so in Paris with a Breton family; but had been too home-sick to remain longer away from the hilly and green country, set in a barren circle of rocks and sands, where she had been born. She thought that one of the boys ought perhaps to be a priest, but said nothing to her husband, who was a republican, and hated the "crows," as he called the ministers of religion. The christening was a splendid affair. All the commune came to it, for the Bacadous were rich and influential, and, now and then, did not mind the expense. The grandfather had a new coat.

Some months afterwards, one evening when the kitchen had been swept, and the door locked, Jean-Pierre, looking at the cot, asked his wife: "What's the matter with those children?" And, as if these words, spoken calmly, had been the portent of misfortune, she answered with a loud wail that must have been heard across the yard in the pig-sty; for the pigs (the Bacadous had the finest pigs in the country) stirred and grunted complainingly in the night. The husband went on grinding his bread and butter slowly, gazing at the wall, the soup-plate smoking under his chin.

He had returned late from the market, where he had overheard (not for the first time) whispers behind his back. He revolved the words in his mind as he drove back. "Simple! Both of them. . . . Never any use! . . . Well! May be, may be. One must see. Would ask his wife." This was her answer. He felt like a blow on his chest, but said only: "Go, draw me some cider. I am thirsty!"

She went out moaning, an empty jug in her hand. Then he arose, took up the light, and moved slowly towards the cradle. They slept. He looked at them sideways, finished his mouthful there, went back heavily, and sat down before his plate. When his wife returned he never looked up, but swallowed a couple of spoonfuls noisily, and remarked, in a dull manner □

"When they sleep they are like other people's children."

She sat down suddenly on a stool near by, and shook with a silent tempest of sobs, unable to speak. He finished his meal, and remained idly thrown back in his chair, his eyes lost amongst the black rafters of the ceiling. Before him the tallow candle flared red and straight, sending up a slender thread of smoke. The light lay on the rough, sunburnt skin of his throat; the sunk cheeks were like patches of darkness, and his aspect was mournfully stolid, as if he had ruminated with difficulty endless ideas. Then he said, deliberately □

"We must see . . . consult people. Don't cry. . . . They won't all be like that . . . surely! We must sleep now."

After the third child, also a boy, was born, Jean-Pierre went about his work with tense hopefulness. His lips seemed more narrow, more tightly compressed than before; as if for fear of letting the earth he tilled hear the voice of hope that murmured within his breast. He watched the child, stepping up to the cot with a heavy clang of sabots on the stone floor, and glanced in, along his shoulder, with that indifference which is like a deformity of peasant humanity. Like the earth they master and serve, those men, slow of eye and speech, do not show the inner fire; so that, at last, it becomes a question with them as with the earth, what there is in the core: heat, violence, a force mysterious and terrible □ or nothing but a clod, a mass fertile and inert, cold and unfeeling, ready to bear a crop of plants that sustain life or give death.

The mother watched with other eyes; listened with otherwise expectant ears. Under the high hanging shelves supporting great sides of bacon overhead, her body was busy by the great fireplace, attentive to the pot swinging on iron gallows, scrubbing the long table where the field hands would sit down directly to their evening meal. Her mind remained by the cradle, night and day on the watch, to hope and suffer. That child, like the other two, never smiled, never stretched its hands to her, never spoke; never had a glance of recognition for her in its big black eyes, which could only stare fixedly at any glitter, but failed hopelessly to follow the brilliance of a sun-ray slipping slowly along the floor. When the men were at work she spent long days between her three idiot children and the childish grandfather, who sat grim, angular, and immovable, with his feet near the warm ashes of the fire. The feeble old fellow seemed to suspect that there was something wrong with his grandsons. Only once, moved either by affection or by the sense of proprieties, he attempted to nurse the youngest. He took the boy up from the floor, clicked his tongue at him, and essayed a shaky gallop of his bony knees. Then he looked closely with his misty eyes at the child's face and deposited him down gently on the floor again. And he sat, his lean shanks crossed, nodding at the steam escaping from the cooking-pot with a gaze senile and worried.

Then mute affliction dwelt in Bacadou's farmhouse, sharing the breath and the bread of its inhabitants; and the priest of the Ploumar parish had great cause for congratulation. He called upon the rich landowner, the Marquis de Chavanes, on purpose to deliver himself with joyful unction of solemn platitudes about the inscrutable ways of Providence. In the vast dimness of the curtained drawing-room, the little man, resembling a black bolster, leaned towards a couch, his hat on his knees, and gesticulated with a fat hand at the elongated, gracefully-flowing lines of the clear Parisian toilette from which the half-amused, half-bored marquise listened with gracious languor. He was exulting and humble, proud and awed. The impossible had come to pass. Jean-Pierre Bacadou, the enraged republican farmer, had been to mass last Sunday □ had proposed to entertain the visiting priests at the next festival of Ploumar! It was a triumph for the Church and for the good cause. "I thought I would come at once to tell Monsieur le Marquis. I know how anxious he is for the welfare of our country," declared the priest, wiping his face. He was asked to stay to dinner.

The Chavanes returning that evening, after seeing their

guest to the main gate of the park, discussed the matter while they strolled in the moonlight, trailing their long shadows up the straight avenue of chestnuts. The marquise, a royalist of course, had been mayor of the commune which includes Ploumar, the scattered hamlets of the coast, and the stony islands that fringe the yellow flatness of the sands. He had felt his position insecure, for there was a strong republican element in that part of the country; but now the conversion of Jean-Pierre made him safe. He was very pleased. "You have no idea how influential those people are," he explained to his wife. "Now, I am sure, the next communal election will go all right. I shall be re- elected." "Your ambition is perfectly insatiable, Charles," exclaimed the marquise, gaily. "But, ma chere amie," argued the husband, seriously, "it's most important that the right man should be mayor this year, because of the elections to the Chamber. If you think it amuses me . . ."

Jean-Pierre had surrendered to his wife's mother. Madame Levaille was a woman of business, known and respected within a radius of at least fifteen miles. Thick-set and stout, she was seen about the country, on foot or in an acquaintance's cart, perpetually moving, in spite of her fifty-eight years, in steady pursuit of business. She had houses in all the hamlets, she worked quarries of granite, she freighted coasters with stone □ even traded with the Channel Islands. She was broad-cheeked, wide-eyed, persuasive in speech: carrying her point with the placid and invincible obstinacy of an old woman who knows her own mind. She very seldom slept for two nights together in the same house; and the wayside inns were the best places to inquire in as to her whereabouts. She had either passed, or was expected to pass there at six; or somebody, coming in, had seen her in the morning, or expected to meet her that evening. After the inns that command the roads, the churches were the buildings she frequented most. Men of liberal opinions would induce small children to run into sacred edifices to see whether Madame Levaille was there, and to tell her that so-and-so was in the road waiting to speak to her about potatoes, or flour, or stones, or houses; and she would curtail her devotions, come out blinking and crossing herself into the sunshine; ready to discuss business matters in a calm, sensible way across a table in the kitchen of the inn opposite. Latterly she had stayed for a few days several times with her son-in-law, arguing against sorrow and misfortune with composed face and gentle tones. Jean-Pierre felt the convictions imbibed in the regiment torn out of his breast □ not by arguments but by facts. Striding over his fields he thought it over. There were three of them. Three! All alike! Why? Such things did not happen to everybody □ to nobody he ever heard of. One□might pass. But three! All three. Forever useless, to be fed while he lived and . . . What would become of the land when he died? This must be seen to. He would sacrifice his convictions. One day he told his wife □

"See what your God will do for us. Pay for some masses."

Susan embraced her man. He stood unbending, then turned on his heels and went out. But afterwards, when a black soutane darkened his doorway, he did not object; even offered some cider himself to the priest. He listened to the talk meekly; went to mass between the two women; accomplished what the priest called "his religious duties" at Easter. That morning he felt like a man who had sold his soul. In the afternoon he fought ferociously with an old friend and neighbour who had remarked that the priests had the best of it and were now going to eat the priest-eater. He came home dishevelled and bleeding, and happening to catch sight of his children (they were kept generally out of the way), cursed and swore incoherently, banging the table. Susan wept. Madame Levaille sat serenely unmoved. She assured her daughter that "It will pass;" and taking up her thick umbrella, departed in haste to see after a schooner she was going to load with granite from her quarry.

A year or so afterwards the girl was born. A girl. Jean-Pierre heard of it in the fields, and was so upset by the news that he sat down on the boundary wall and remained there till the evening, instead of going home as he was urged to do. A girl! He felt half cheated. However, when he got home he was partly reconciled to his fate. One could marry her to a good fellow □ not to a good for nothing, but to a fellow with some understanding and a good pair of arms. Besides, the next may be a boy, he thought. Of course they would be all right. His new credulity knew of no doubt. The ill luck was broken. He spoke cheerily to his wife. She was also hopeful. Three priests came to that christening, and Madame Levaille was godmother. The child turned out an idiot too.

Then on market days Jean-Pierre was seen bargaining bitterly, quarrelsome and greedy; then getting drunk with taciturn earnestness; then driving home in the dusk at a rate fit for a wedding, but with a face gloomy enough for a funeral. Sometimes he would insist on his wife coming with him; and they would drive in the early morning, shaking side by side on the narrow seat above the helpless pig, that, with tied legs, grunted a melancholy sigh at every rut. The morning drives were silent; but in the evening, coming home, Jean-Pierre, tipsy, was viciously muttering, and growled at the confounded woman who could not rear children that were like anybody else's. Susan, holding on against the erratic swayings of the cart, pretended not to hear. Once, as they were driving through Ploumar, some obscure and drunken impulse caused him to pull up sharply opposite the church. The moon swam amongst light white clouds. The tombstones gleamed pale under the fretted shadows of the trees in the churchyard. Even the village dogs slept. Only the nightingales, awake, spun out the thrill of their song above the silence of graves. Jean-Pierre said thickly to his wife □

"What do you think is there?"

He pointed his whip at the tower □ in which the big dial of the clock appeared high in the moonlight like a pallid face without eyes □ and getting out carefully, fell down at once by the wheel. He picked himself up and climbed one by one the few steps to the iron gate of the churchyard. He put his face to the bars and called out indistinctly □

"Hey there! Come out!"

"Jean! Return! Return!" entreated his wife in low tones.

He took no notice, and seemed to wait there. The song of nightingales beat on all sides against the high walls of the church, and flowed back between stone crosses and flat gray slabs, engraved with words of hope and sorrow.

"Hey! Come out!" shouted Jean-Pierre, loudly.

The nightingales ceased to sing.

"Nobody?" went on Jean-Pierre. "Nobody there. A swindle of the crows. That's what this is. Nobody anywhere. I despise it. Allez! Houp!"

He shook the gate with all his strength, and the iron bars rattled with a frightful clanging, like a chain dragged over stone steps. A dog near by barked hurriedly. Jean-Pierre staggered back, and after three successive dashes got into his cart. Susan sat very quiet and still. He said to her with drunken severity □

"See? Nobody. I've been made a fool! Malheur! Somebody will pay for it. The next one I see near the house I will lay my whip on . . . on the black spine . . . I will. I don't want him in there . . . he only helps the carrion crows to rob poor folk. I am a man. . . . We will see if I can't have children like anybody else . . . now you mind. . . . They won't be all . . . all . . . we see. . . ."

She burst out through the fingers that hid her face □

"Don't say that, Jean; don't say that, my man!"

He struck her a swinging blow on the head with the back of his hand and knocked her into the bottom of the cart, where she crouched, thrown about lamentably by every jolt. He drove furiously, standing up, brandishing his whip, shaking the reins over the gray horse that galloped ponderously, making the heavy harness leap upon his broad quarters. The country rang clamorous in the night with the irritated barking of farm dogs, that followed the rattle of wheels all along the road. A couple of belated wayfarers had only just time to step into the ditch. At his own gate he caught the post and was shot out of the cart head first. The horse went on slowly to the door. At Susan's piercing cries the farm hands rushed out. She thought him dead, but he was only sleeping where he fell, and cursed his men, who hastened to him, for disturbing his slumbers.

Autumn came. The clouded sky descended low upon the black contours of the hills; and the dead leaves danced in spiral whirls under naked trees, till the wind, sighing profoundly, laid them to rest in the hollows of bare valleys. And from morning till night one could see all over the land black denuded boughs, the boughs gnarled and twisted, as if contorted with pain, swaying sadly between the wet clouds and the soaked earth. The clear and gentle streams of summer days rushed discoloured and raging at the stones that barred the way to the sea, with the fury of madness bent upon suicide. From horizon to horizon the great road to the sands lay between the hills in a dull glitter of empty curves, resembling an unnavigable river of mud.

Jean-Pierre went from field to field, moving blurred and tall in the drizzle, or striding on the crests of rises, lonely and high upon the gray curtain of drifting clouds, as if he had been pacing along the very edge of the universe. He looked at the black earth, at the earth mute and promising, at the mysterious earth doing its work of life in death-like stillness under the veiled sorrow of the sky. And it seemed to him that to a man worse than childless there was no promise in the fertility of fields, that from him the earth escaped, defied him, frowned at him like the clouds, sombre and hurried above his head. Having to face alone his own fields, he felt the inferiority of man who passes away before the clod that remains. Must he give up the hope of having by his side a son who would look at the turned-up sods with a master's eye? A man that would think as he thought, that would feel as he felt; a man who would be part of himself, and yet remain to trample masterfully on that earth when he was gone? He thought of some distant relations, and felt savage enough to curse them aloud. They! Never! He turned homewards, going straight at the roof of his dwelling, visible between the enlaced skeletons of trees. As he swung his legs over the stile a cawing flock of birds settled slowly on the field; dropped down behind his back, noiseless and fluttering, like flakes of soot.

That day Madame Levaille had gone early in the afternoon to the house she had near Kervanion. She had to pay some of the men who worked in her granite quarry there, and she went in good time because her little house contained a shop where the workmen could spend their wages without the trouble of going to town. The house stood alone amongst rocks. A lane of mud and stones ended at the door. The sea-winds coming ashore on Stonecutter's point, fresh from the fierce turmoil of the waves, howled violently at the unmoved heaps of black boulders holding up steadily short-armed, high crosses against the tremendous rush of the invisible. In the sweep of gales the sheltered dwelling stood in a calm resonant and disquieting, like the calm in the centre of a hurricane.

On stormy nights, when the tide was out, the bay of Fougere, fifty feet below the house, resembled an immense black pit, from which ascended mutterings and sighs as if the sands down there had been alive and complaining. At high tide the returning water assaulted the ledges of rock in short rushes, ending in bursts of livid light and columns of spray, that flew inland, stinging to death the grass of pastures.

The darkness came from the hills, flowed over the coast, put out the red fires of sunset, and went on to seaward pursuing the retiring tide. The wind dropped with the sun, leaving a maddened sea and a devastated sky. The heavens above the house seemed to be draped in black rags, held up here and there by pins of fire. Madame Levaille, for this evening the servant of her own workmen, tried to induce them to depart. "An old woman like me ought to be in bed at this late hour," she good-humouredly repeated. The quarrymen drank, asked for more. They shouted over the table as if they had been talking across a field. At one end four of them played cards, banging the wood with their hard knuckles, and swearing at every lead. One sat with a lost gaze, humming a bar of some song, which he repeated endlessly. Two others, in a corner, were quarrelling confidentially and fiercely over some woman, looking close into one another's eyes as if they had wanted to tear them out, but speaking in whispers that promised violence and murder discreetly, in a venomous sibillation of subdued words. The atmosphere in there was thick enough to slice with a knife. Three candles burning about the long room glowed red and dull like sparks expiring in ashes.

The slight click of the iron latch was at that late hour as unexpected and startling as a thunder-clap. Madame Levaille put down a bottle she held above a liqueur glass; the players turned their heads; the whispered quarrel ceased; only the singer, after darting a glance at the door, went on humming with a stolid face. Susan appeared in the doorway, stepped in, flung the door to, and put her back against it, saying, half aloud □

"Mother!"

Madame Levaille, taking up the bottle again, said calmly: "Here you are, my girl. What a state you are in!" The neck of the bottle rang on the rim of the glass, for the old woman was startled, and the idea that the farm had caught fire had entered her head. She could think of no other cause for her daughter's appearance.

Susan, soaked and muddy, stared the whole length of the room towards the men at the far end. Her mother asked □

"What has happened? God guard us from misfortune!"

Susan moved her lips. No sound came. Madame Levaille stepped up to her daughter, took her by the arm, looked into her face.

"In God's name," she said, shakily, "what's the matter? You have been rolling in mud. . . . Why did you come? . . . Where's Jean?"

The men had all got up and approached slowly, staring with dull surprise. Madame Levaille jerked her daughter away from the door, swung her round upon a seat close to the wall. Then she turned fiercely to the men □

"Enough of this! Out you go □ you others! I close."

One of them observed, looking down at Susan collapsed on the seat: "She is □ one may say □ half dead."

Madame Levaille flung the door open.

"Get out! March!" she cried, shaking nervously.

They dropped out into the night, laughing stupidly. Outside, the two Lotharios broke out into loud shouts. The others tried to soothe them, all talking at once. The noise went away up the lane with the men, who staggered together in a tight knot, remonstrating with one another foolishly.

"Speak, Susan. What is it? Speak!" entreated Madame Levaille, as soon as the door was shut.

Susan pronounced some incomprehensible words, glaring at the table. The old woman clapped her hands above her head, let them drop, and stood looking at her daughter with disconsolate eyes. Her husband had been "deranged in his head" for a few years before he died, and now she began to suspect her daughter was going mad. She asked, pressingly □

"Does Jean know where you are? Where is Jean?"

"He knows . . . he is dead."

"What!" cried the old woman. She came up near, and peering at her daughter, repeated three times: "What do you say? What do you say? What do you say?"

Susan sat dry-eyed and stony before Madame Levaille, who contemplated her, feeling a strange sense of inexplicable horror creep into the silence of the house. She had hardly realised the news, further than to understand that she had been brought in one short moment face to face with something unexpected and final. It did not even occur to her to ask for any explanation. She thought: accident □ terrible accident □ blood to the head □ fell down a trap door in the loft. . . . She remained there, distracted and mute, blinking her old eyes.

Suddenly, Susan said □

"I have killed him."

For a moment the mother stood still, almost unbreathing, but with composed face. The next second she burst out into a shout □

"You miserable madwoman. . . . they will cut your neck. . . ."

She fancied the gendarmes entering the house, saying to her: "We want your daughter; give her up:" the gendarmes with the severe, hard faces of men on duty. She knew the brigadier well □ an old friend, familiar and respectful, saying heartily, "To your good health, Madame!" before lifting to his lips the small glass of cognac □ out of the special bottle she kept for friends. And now! . . . She was losing her head. She rushed here and there, as if looking for something urgently needed □ gave that up, stood stock still in the middle of the room, and screamed at her daughter □

"Why? Say! Say! Why?"

The other seemed to leap out of her strange apathy.

"Do you think I am made of stone?" she shouted back, striding towards her mother.

"No! It's impossible. . . ." said Madame Levaille, in a convinced tone.

"You go and see, mother," retorted Susan, looking at her with blazing eyes. "There's no money in heaven □ no justice. No! . . . I did not know. . . . Do you think I have no heart? Do you think I have never heard people jeering at me, pitying me, wondering at me? Do you know how some of them were calling me? The mother of idiots — that was my nickname! And my children never would know me, never speak to me. They would know nothing; neither men — nor God. Haven't I prayed! But the Mother of God herself would not hear me. A mother! . . . Who is accursed — I, or the man who is dead? Eh? Tell me. I took care of myself. Do you think I would defy the anger of God and have my house full of those things — that are worse than animals who know the hand that feeds them? Who blasphemed in the night at the very church door? Was it I? . . . I only wept and prayed for mercy . . . and I feel the curse at every moment of the day — I see it round me from morning to night . . . I've got to keep them alive — to take care of my misfortune and shame. And he would come. I begged him and Heaven for mercy. . . . No! . . . Then we shall see. . . . He came this evening. I thought to myself: 'Ah! again!' . . . I had my long scissors. I heard him shouting . . . I saw him near. . . . I must — must I? . . . Then take! . . . And I struck him in the throat above the breastbone. . . . I never heard him even sigh. . . . I left him standing. . . . It was a minute ago. How did I come here?"

Madame Levaille shivered. A wave of cold ran down her back, down her fat arms under her tight sleeves, made her stamp gently where she stood. Quivers ran over the broad cheeks, across the thin lips, ran amongst the wrinkles at the corners of her steady old eyes. She stammered —

"You wicked woman — you disgrace me. But there! You

always resembled your father. What do you think will become of you . . . in the other world? In this . . . Oh misery!"

She was very hot now. She felt burning inside. She wrung her perspiring hands □ and suddenly, starting in great haste, began to look for her big shawl and umbrella, feverishly, never once glancing at her daughter, who stood in the middle of the room following her with a gaze distracted and cold.

"Nothing worse than in this," said Susan.

Her mother, umbrella in hand and trailing the shawl over the floor, groaned profoundly.

"I must go to the priest," she burst out passionately. "I do not know whether you even speak the truth! You are a horrible woman. They will find you anywhere. You may stay here □ or go. There is no room for you in this world."

Ready now to depart, she yet wandered aimlessly about the room, putting the bottles on the shelf, trying to fit with trembling hands the covers on cardboard boxes. Whenever the real sense of what she had heard emerged for a second from the haze of her thoughts she would fancy that something had exploded in her brain without, unfortunately, bursting her head to pieces □ which would have been a relief. She blew the candles out one by one without knowing it, and was horribly startled by the darkness. She fell on a bench and began to whimper. After a while she ceased, and sat listening to the breathing of her daughter, whom she could hardly see, still and upright, giving no other sign of life. She was becoming old rapidly at last, during those minutes. She spoke in tones unsteady, cut about by the rattle of teeth, like one shaken by a deadly cold fit of ague.

"I wish you had died little. I will never dare to show my old head in the sunshine again. There are worse misfortunes than idiot children. I wish you had been born to me simple □ like your own. . . ."

She saw the figure of her daughter pass before the faint and livid clearness of a window. Then it appeared in the doorway for a second, and the door swung to with a clang. Madame Levaille, as if awakened by the noise from a long nightmare, rushed out.

"Susan!" she shouted from the doorstep.

She heard a stone roll a long time down the declivity of the rocky beach above the sands. She stepped forward cautiously, one hand on the wall of the house, and peered down into the smooth darkness of the empty bay. Once again she cried □

"Susan! You will kill yourself there."

The stone had taken its last leap in the dark, and she heard nothing now. A sudden thought seemed to strangle her, and she called no more. She turned her back upon the black silence of the pit and went up the lane towards Ploumar, stumbling along with sombre determination, as if she had started on a desperate journey that would last, perhaps, to the end of her life. A sullen and periodic clamour of waves rolling over reefs followed her far inland between the high hedges sheltering the gloomy solitude of the fields.

Susan had run out, swerving sharp to the left at the door, and on the edge of the slope crouched down behind a boulder. A dislodged stone went on downwards, rattling as it leaped. When Madame Levaille called out, Susan could have, by stretching her hand, touched her mother's skirt, had she had the courage to move a limb. She saw the old woman go away, and she remained still, closing her eyes and pressing her side to the hard and rugged surface of the rock. After a while a familiar face with fixed eyes and an open mouth became visible in the intense obscurity amongst the boulders. She uttered a low cry and stood up. The face vanished, leaving her to gasp and shiver alone in the wilderness of stone heaps. But as soon as she had crouched down again to rest, with her head against the rock, the face returned, came very near, appeared eager to finish the speech that had been cut short by death, only a moment ago. She scrambled quickly to her feet and said: "Go away, or I will do it again." The thing wavered, swung to the right, to the left. She moved this way and that, stepped back, fancied herself screaming at it, and was appalled by the unbroken stillness of the night. She tottered on the brink, felt the steep declivity under her feet, and rushed down blindly to save herself from a headlong fall. The shingle seemed to wake up; the pebbles began to roll before her, pursued her from above, raced down with her on both sides, rolling past with an increasing clatter. In the peace of the night the noise grew, deepening to a rumour, continuous and violent, as if the whole semicircle of the stony beach had started to tumble down into the bay. Susan's feet hardly touched the slope that seemed to run down with her. At the bottom she stumbled, shot forward, throwing her arms out, and fell heavily. She jumped up at once and turned swiftly to look back, her clenched hands full of sand she had clutched in her fall. The face was there, keeping its distance, visible in its own sheen that made a pale stain in the night. She shouted, "Go away!" □ she shouted at it with pain, with fear, with all the rage of that useless stab that could not keep him quiet, keep him out of her sight. What did he want now? He was dead. Dead men have no children. Would he never leave her alone? She shrieked at it □ waved her outstretched hands. She seemed to feel the breath of parted lips, and, with a long cry of discouragement, fled across the level bottom of the bay.

She ran lightly, unaware of any effort of her body. High sharp rocks that, when the bay is full, show above the glittering plain of blue water like pointed towers of submerged churches, glided past her, rushing to the land at a tremendous pace. To the left, in the distance, she could see something shining: a broad disc of light in which narrow shadows pivoted round the centre like the spokes of a wheel. She heard a voice calling, "Hey! There!" and answered with a wild scream. So, he could call yet! He was calling after her to stop. Never! . . . She tore through the night, past the startled group of seaweed-gatherers who stood round their lantern paralysed with fear at the unearthly screech coming from that fleeing shadow. The men leaned on their pitchforks staring fearfully. A woman fell on her knees, and, crossing herself, began to pray aloud. A little girl with her ragged skirt full of slimy seaweed began to sob despairingly, lugging her soaked burden close to the man who carried the light. Somebody said: “The thing ran out towards the sea.” Another voice exclaimed: “And the sea is coming back! Look at the spreading puddles. Do you hear □ you woman □ there! Get up!” Several voices cried together. “Yes, let us be off! Let the accursed thing go to the sea!” They moved on, keeping close round the light. Suddenly a man swore loudly. He would go and see what was the matter. It had been a woman's voice. He would go. There were shrill protests from women □ but his high form detached itself from the group and went off running. They sent an unanimous call of scared voices after him. A word, insulting and mocking, came back, thrown at them through the darkness. A woman moaned. An old man said gravely: “Such things ought to be left alone.” They went on slower, shuffling in the yielding sand and whispering to one another that Millot feared nothing, having no religion, but that it would end badly some day.

Susan met the incoming tide by the Raven islet and stopped, panting, with her feet in the water. She heard the murmur and felt the cold caress of the sea, and, calmer now, could see the sombre and confused mass of the Raven on one side and on the other the long white streak of Molene sands that are left high above the dry bottom of Fougere Bay at every ebb. She turned round and saw far away, along the starred background of the sky, the ragged outline of the coast. Above it, nearly facing her, appeared the tower of Ploumar Church; a slender and tall pyramid shooting up dark and pointed into the clustered glitter of the stars. She felt strangely calm. She knew where she was, and began to remember how she came there □ and why.

She peered into the smooth obscurity near her. She was alone. There was nothing there; nothing near her, either living or dead.

The tide was creeping in quietly, putting out long impatient arms of strange rivulets that ran towards the land between ridges of sand. Under the night the pools grew bigger with mysterious rapidity, while the great sea, yet far off, thundered in a regular rhythm along the indistinct line of the horizon. Susan splashed her way back for a few yards without being able to get clear of the water that murmured tenderly all around and, suddenly, with a spiteful gurgle, nearly took her off her feet. Her heart thumped with fear. This place was too big and too empty to die in. To-morrow they would do with her what they liked. But before she died she must tell them □ tell the gentlemen in black clothes that there are things no woman can bear. She must explain how it happened. . . . She splashed through a pool, getting wet to the waist, too preoccupied to care. . . . She must explain. "He came in the same way as ever and said, just so: 'Do you think I am going to leave the land to those people from Morbihan that I do not know? Do you? We shall see! Come along, you creature of mischance!' And he put his arms out. Then, Messieurs, I said: 'Before God □ never!' And he said, striding at me with open palms: 'There is no God to hold me! Do you understand, you useless carcase. I will do what I like.' And he took me by the shoulders. Then I, Messieurs, called to God for help, and next minute, while he was shaking me, I felt my long scissors in my hand. His shirt was unbuttoned, and, by the candle-light, I saw the hollow of his throat. I cried: 'Let go!' He was crushing my shoulders. He was strong, my man was! Then I thought: No! . . . Must I? . . . Then take! □ and I struck in the hollow place. I never saw him fall. . . . The old father never turned his head. He is deaf and childish, gentlemen. . . . Nobody saw him fall. I ran out . . . Nobody saw. . . ."

She had been scrambling amongst the boulders of the Raven and now found herself, all out of breath, standing amongst the heavy shadows of the rocky islet. The Raven is connected with the main land by a natural pier of immense and slippery stones. She intended to return home that way. Was he still standing there? At home. Home! Four idiots and a corpse. She must go back and explain. Anybody would understand. . . .

Below her the night or the sea seemed to pronounce distinctly □

"Aha! I see you at last!"

She started, slipped, fell; and without attempting to rise, listened, terrified. She heard heavy breathing, a clatter of wooden clogs. It stopped.

"Where the devil did you pass?" said an invisible man, hoarsely.

She held her breath. She recognized the voice. She had not seen him fall. Was he pursuing her there dead, or perhaps . . . alive?

She lost her head. She cried from the crevice where she lay huddled, "Never, never!"

"Ah! You are still there. You led me a fine dance. Wait, my beauty, I must see how you look after all this. You wait. . . ."

Millot was stumbling, laughing, swearing meaninglessly out of pure satisfaction, pleased with himself for having run down that fly-by-night. "As if there were such things as ghosts! Bah! It took an old African soldier to show those clodhoppers. . . . But it was curious. Who the devil was she?"

Susan listened, crouching. He was coming for her, this dead man. There was no escape. What a noise he made amongst the stones. . . . She saw his head rise up, then the shoulders. He was tall □ her own man! His long arms waved about, and it was his own voice sounding a little strange . . . because of the scissors. She scrambled out quickly, rushed to the edge of the causeway, and turned round. The man stood still on a high stone, detaching himself in dead black on the glitter of the sky.

"Where are you going to?" he called, roughly.

She answered, "Home!" and watched him intensely. He made a striding, clumsy leap on to another boulder, and stopped again, balancing himself, then said □

"Ha! ha! Well, I am going with you. It's the least I can do. Ha! ha! ha!"

She stared at him till her eyes seemed to become glowing coals that burned deep into her brain, and yet she was in mortal fear of making out the well-known features. Below her the sea lapped softly against the rock with a splash continuous and gentle.

The man said, advancing another step □

"I am coming for you. What do you think?"

She trembled. Coming for her! There was no escape, no peace, no hope. She looked round despairingly. Suddenly the whole shadowy coast, the blurred islets, the heaven itself, swayed about twice, then came to a rest. She closed her eyes and shouted □

"Can't you wait till I am dead!"

She was shaken by a furious hate for that shade that pursued her in this world, unappeased even by death in its longing for an heir that would be like other people's children.

Hey! What?" said Millot, keeping his distance prudently. He was saying to himself: "Look out! Some lunatic. An accident happens soon."

She went on, wildly □

"I want to live. To live alone □ for a week □ for a day. I must explain to them. . . . I would tear you to pieces, I would kill you twenty times over rather than let you touch me while I live. How many times must I kill you □ you blasphemer! Satan sends you here. I am damned too!"

"Come," said Millot, alarmed and conciliating. "I am perfectly alive! . . . Oh, my God!"

She had screamed, "Alive!" and at once vanished before his eyes, as if the islet itself had swerved aside from under her feet. Millot rushed forward, and fell flat with his chin over the edge. Far below he saw the water whitened by her struggles, and heard one shrill cry for help that seemed to dart upwards along the perpendicular face of the rock, and soar past, straight into the high and impassive heaven.

Madame Levaille sat, dry-eyed, on the short grass of the hill side, with her thick legs stretched out, and her old feet turned up in their black cloth shoes. Her clogs stood near by, and further off the umbrella lay on the withered sward like a weapon dropped from the grasp of a vanquished warrior. The Marquis of Chavanes, on horseback, one gloved hand on thigh, looked down at her as she got up laboriously, with groans. On the narrow track of the seaweed-carts four men were carrying inland Susan's body on a hand-barrow, while several others straggled listlessly behind. Madame Levaille looked after the procession. "Yes, Monsieur le Marquis," she said dispassionately, in her usual calm tone of a reasonable old woman. "There are unfortunate people on this earth. I had only one child. Only one! And they won't bury her in consecrated ground!"

Her eyes filled suddenly, and a short shower of tears rolled down the broad cheeks. She pulled the shawl close about her. The Marquis leaned slightly over in his saddle, and said □

"It is very sad. You have all my sympathy. I shall speak to the Cure. She was unquestionably insane, and the fall was accidental. Millot says so distinctly. Good-day, Madame."

And he trotted off, thinking to himself: "I must get this old woman appointed guardian of those idiots, and administrator of the farm. It would be much better than having here one of those other Bacadous, probably a red republican, corrupting my commune."

EXPLANATION OF
Words & Idioms

Biniou: (French) bagpipe.

Bolster: (n) a long narrow cushion.

Brigadier: (n) a high ranking military position below a general.

Brusque: (adj) sudden manner of speech.

Cider: (n) a juice or alcohol made from fruit juice.

Christening: (n) the baptizing and giving a name to a child in the Christian church.

Coaster: (n) a giant sled.

Commune: (n) a group of people in a small community that share everything.

Cot: (n) British for crib.

Cure: (n) a priest in the Catholic Church.

Curtail: (v) limit.

Daubs: (n) an amateurish painting.

Emaciated: (adj) very thin to point of looking starved.

Essay: (v) try.

Furze: (n) a thick type of shrub.

Gallows: (n) a crossbar over a fire that a cooking pot hangs from.

Gendarmes: (n) French national police, part of the army.

Imbibe: (v) to receive into the mind.

Inexplicable: (adj) difficult to explain.

Languor: (n) not having any energy.

Lotharios: (n) a playboy.

Ma chere amie: (French) My dear friend.

Malheur! (French) Misfortune.

Maraud: (v) to wander around in search of something valuable.

Marquis: (n) Title of a French nobleman.

Meager: (adj) lacking quantity.

Nurse: (v) to feed a baby from the breast.

Recalcitrant: (adj) stubborn.

Regiment: (n) self-control.

Remonstrate: (v) to speak in protest.

Republican: (n) a person who does not support a king or monarch but the rule of the people under an elected official.

Rheumatism: (n) a pain the muscles and joints.

Royalist: (n) a person who supports a king or a monarch.

Ruminate: (v) to think a matter over carefully.

Sabot: (n) a wooden shoe.

Schooner: (n) a covered wagon used for hauling freight.

Shanks: (n) legs.

Sibillation: (n) a hissing sound.

Soutane: (n) the black clothing worn by a priest.

Stile: (n) steps that go up and down a rock fence.

Stolidly: (adv) without emotion.

Taciturn: (adj) untalkative.

Tallow: (n) the white fat from cattle that is used to make candles.

Throng: (v) to crowd into

Undulate: (v) to move up and down in a wave-like motion.

Wringing tribute: (v) to obtain something through hard work.

Study Questions

1. The title of the story is "The Idiots." Does this apply just to the children? Explain your answer.

2. Joseph Conrad is famous for creating characters suffering from self-deception. How do the three main characters, Jean-Pierre, Susan, and Madame Levaille suffer from self-deception? Give examples from the story to support your answer.

3. The setting of a story is often used to mirror the current mood of the characters. Give some examples of how Conrad uses setting to establish mood with his three main characters.

4. The narrator is briefly introduced at the beginning of the story and never "seen" again. He never sees any of the events first hand. He relates to the reader only what he has heard. Why even introduce such a narrator? What is the literary purpose of having a disconnected narrator? In what ways is such a narrator effective in telling this type of a story?

5. If the narrator only heard his story from scattered accounts and then retells it to the reader, can the narrator be trusted with his story?

6. The narrator speaks of his story as "a tale formidable and simple, as they always are, those disclosures of obscure trials endured by ignorant hearts." Is his tale really a simple one? Why or why not? Can the characters in the story be considered ignorant?

IX. THE LAST LESSON

by Alphonse Daudet

INTRODUCTION OF THE AUTHOR:
Alphonse Daudet (1840-1897)

Alphonse Daudet (pronounced *doe-day*) was a very prolific French writer who was born in Nimes in 1840. He wrote his first novel when he was only 14, yet his education was often incomplete; he was usually a truant student and suffered from depression. Not a family with money to begin with, Daudet's father fell into debt, forcing Daudet, at the age of 16, to take the position of study master at a local school; a position he did not greatly care for. With unruly, loud children, Daudet would often wake in the middle of night in a cold sweat with memories still of being surrounded by rowdy pupils. Yet his love for writing would eventually rescue him when he finally moved to Paris a year later to publish a small volume of poems *Les Amoureuses* (1858, tr. *Women in Love*). He secured his writing career with the publication of a collection of short stories *Lettres de mon moulin* (1869, tr. *Letters from My Mill*). Most of his writing is marked by witty or ironic humor, as well as having a taste of the autobiographical, as can be seen in his short story "La Dernière Classe" (1875, tr. "The Last Lesson"), which shows his desire for students to understand the importance of studying.

While he obtained fame and a notable lifestyle as a writer, Daudet was also appointed secretary of the Duke of Morny, the half brother and an all powerful minister of Napoleon III (Napoleon's grandson); a post he held until Morny's death in 1865 and secured him a small fortune. In 1867, he married Julia Allard, a woman of like intelligence and writing ability. His literary career picked up steam after his service as the Duke's secretary and he went on to further fame and fortune by publishing plays and letters. His literary success finally came with the publication of *Fromont Jeune et Risler Aine* (1874, tr. Fr*omont the Younger and Riler the Elder*) that won him honors from the French Academy.

In 1870, Daudet enlisted in the army to fight in the Franco-Prussian War (July 19, 1870 □ May 10, 1871), which was instigated by France's Napoleon III's concern over a German prince crowned in Spain and his efforts to stop it. The results of which led to France declaring war on Prussia (which was a German state at the time). Six months later, German forces overwhelmed the French, and Napoleon III was captured followed by Paris falling. This was, of course, a great embarrassment to the French who had ruled most of Europe as a grand empire and effected the everyday lives of the proud French as is also illustrated in "The Last Lesson." France had lost its second empire and was forced into a republic that lasted up until the end of hostilities in World War II. In 1873, Daudet published a collection of patriotic short stories *Contes du Lundi* that includes "The Last Lesson."

Alphonse Daudet suffered from insomnia and then syphilis that eventually overcame him. He recorded his agonizing ordeal in diaries that were not collected and published until 1930 in *La Doulou* (tr. *In the Land of Pain*). He died in Paris, France on December 16, 1897.

Synopsis

The narrator, a rather inattentive young boy, starts for school with the dread of most school children □ he did not do his homework. Instead of facing the anger of his schoolmaster, he is tempted with the idea of playing hooky and enjoying the beautiful summer day outside. But commonsense gets the better of him and he heads for school, passing the Prussian soldiers practicing drills and a commotion of people reading bad news posted on the bulletin board outside the town hall.

When he reaches school late, he already notices that it is quiet and peaceful without a sound of screaming or talking, and his teacher, Monsieur Hamel, is not even angry for his tardiness. He even notices some of the older town gentlemen sitting in the back. Then the bad news comes. Germany has overcome France, and all must learn German instead of their native French. This will be their last French lesson. The reason M. Hamel is all dressed in his finest, the older town gentlemen in attendance, and the uncanny attentiveness of all the children suddenly makes painful sense. All feel the regret for taking advantage of the freedom they had to learn their language at a leisurely pace and not even take it seriously. One never knows what one has until it is gone. The schoolmaster teaches all the lessons fully, even though they won't continue tomorrow but be replaced with German lessons.

The final comment the old schoolmaster leaves his pupils is his wish for the respect of language, his wish for freedom. "Vive la France!"

TEXT

I started for school very late that morning and was in great dread of a scolding, especially because M. Hamel had said that he would question us on participles, and I did not know the first word about them. For a moment I thought of running away and spending the day out of doors. It was so warm, so bright! The birds were chirping at the edge of the woods; and in the open field back of the sawmill the Prussian soldiers were drilling. It was all much more tempting than the rule for participles, but I had the strength to resist, and hurried off to school.

When I passed the town hall there was a crowd in front of the bulletin-board. For the last two years all our bad news had come from there □ the lost battles, the draft, the orders of the commanding officer □ and I thought to myself, without stopping:

"What can be the matter now?"

Then, as I hurried by as fast as I could go, the blacksmith, Wachter, who was there, with his apprentice, reading the bulletin, called after me:

"Don't go so fast, bub; you'll get to your school in plenty of time!"

I thought he was making fun of me, and reached M. Hamel's little garden all out of breath.

Usually, when school began, there was a great bustle, which could be heard out in the street, the opening and closing of desks, lessons repeated in unison, very loud, with our hands over our ears to understand better, and the teacher's great ruler rapping on the table. But now it was all so still! I had counted on the commotion to get to my desk without being seen; but, of course, that day everything had to be as quiet as Sunday morning. Through the window I saw my classmates, already in their places, and M. Hamel walking up and down with his terrible iron ruler under his arm. I had to open the door and go in before everybody. You can imagine how I blushed and how frightened I was.

But nothing happened. M. Hamel saw me and said very kindly:

"Go to your place quickly, little Franz. We were beginning without you."

I jumped over the bench and sat down at my desk. Not till then, when I had got a little over my fright, did I see that our teacher had on his beautiful green coat, his frilled shirt, and the little black silk cap, all embroidered, that he never wore except on inspection and prize days. Besides, the whole school seemed so strange and solemn. But the thing that surprised me most was to see, on the back benches that were always empty, the village people sitting quietly like ourselves; old Hauser, with his three-cornered hat, the former mayor, the former postmaster, and several others besides. Everybody looked sad; and Hauser had brought an old primer, thumbed at the edges, and he held it open on his knees with his great spectacles lying across the pages.

While I was wondering about it all, M. Hamel mounted his chair, and, in the same grave and gentle tone which he had used to me, said:

"My children, this is the last lesson I shall give you. The order has come from Berlin to teach only German in the schools of Alsace and Lorraine. The new master comes to-morrow. This is your last French lesson. I want you to be very attentive."

What a thunderclap these words were to me!

Oh, the wretches; that was what they had put up at the town-hall!

My last French lesson! Why, I hardly knew how to write! I should never learn any more! I must stop there, then! Oh, how sorry I was for not learning my lessons, for seeking birds' eggs, or going sliding on the Saar! My books, that had seemed such a nuisance a while ago, so heavy to carry, my grammar, and my history of the saints, were old friends now that I couldn't give up. And M. Hamel, too; the idea that he was going away, that I should never see him again, made me forget all about his ruler and how cranky he was.

Poor man! It was in honor of this last lesson that he had put on his fine Sunday clothes, and now I understood why the old men of the village were sitting there in the back of the room. It was because they were sorry, too, that they had not gone to school more. It was their way of thanking our master for his forty years of faithful service and of showing their respect for the country that was theirs no more.

While I was thinking of all this, I heard my name called. It was my turn to recite. What would I not have given to be able to say that dreadful rule for the participle all through, very loud and clear, and without one mistake? But I got mixed up on the first words and stood there, holding on to my desk, my heart beating, and not daring to look up. I heard M. Hamel say to me:

"I won't scold you, little Franz; you must feel bad enough. See how it is! Every day we have said to ourselves: 'Bah! I've plenty of time. I'll learn it to-morrow.' And now you see where we've come out. Ah, that's the great trouble with Alsace; she puts off learning till to-morrow. Now those fellows out there will have the right to say to you: 'How is it; you pretend to be Frenchmen, and yet you can neither speak nor write your own language?' But you are not the worst, poor little Franz. We've all a great deal to reproach ourselves with.

"Your parents were not anxious enough to have you learn. They preferred to put you to work on a farm or at the mills, so as to have a little more money. And I? I've been to blame also. Have I not often sent you to water my flowers instead of learning your lessons? And when I wanted to go fishing, did I not just give you a holiday?"

Then, from one thing to another, M. Hamel went on to talk of the French language, saying that it was the most beautiful language in the world □ the clearest, the most logical; that we must guard it among us and never forget it, because when a people are enslaved, as long as they hold fast to their language it is as if they had the key to their prison. Then he opened a grammar and read us our lesson. I was amazed to see how well I understood it. All he said seemed so easy, so easy! I think, too, that I had never listened so carefully, and that he had never explained everything with so much patience. It seemed almost as if the poor man wanted to give us all he knew before going away, and to put it all into our heads at one stroke.

After the grammar, we had a lesson in writing. That day M. Hamel had new copies for us, written in a beautiful round hand: France, Alsace, France, Alsace. They looked like little flags floating everywhere in the school-room, hung from the rod at the top of our desks. You ought to have seen how every one set to work, and how quiet it was! The only sound was the scratching of the pens over the paper. Once some beetles flew in; but nobody paid any attention to them, not even the littlest ones, who worked right on tracing their fish-hooks, as if that was French, too. On the roof the pigeons cooed very low, and I thought to myself:

"Will they make them sing in German, even the pigeons?"

Whenever I looked up from my writing I saw M. Hamel sitting motionless in his chair and gazing first at one thing, then at another, as if he wanted to fix in his mind just how everything looked in that little school-room. Fancy! For forty years he had been there in the same place, with his garden outside the window and his class in front of him, just like that. Only the desks and benches had been worn smooth; the walnut-trees in the garden were taller, and the hopvine that he had planted himself twined about the windows to the roof. How it must have broken his heart to leave it all, poor man; to hear his sister moving about in the room above, packing their trunks! For they must leave the country next day.

But he had the courage to hear every lesson to the very

last. After the writing, we had a lesson in history, and then the babies chanted their ba, be bi, bo, bu. Down there at the back of the room old Hauser had put on his spectacles and, holding his primer in both hands, spelled the letters with them. You could see that he, too, was crying; his voice trembled with emotion, and it was so funny to hear him that we all wanted to laugh and cry. Ah, how well I remember it, that last lesson!

All at once the church-clock struck twelve. Then the Angelus. At the same moment the trumpets of the Prussians, returning from drill, sounded under our windows. M. Hamel stood up, very pale, in his chair. I never saw him look so tall.

"My friends," said he, "I □ I □" But something choked him. He could not go on.

Then he turned to the blackboard, took a piece of chalk, and, bearing on with all his might, he wrote as large as he could:

"Vive La France!"

Then he stopped and leaned his head against the wall, and, without a word, he made a gesture to us with his hand:

"School is dismissed □ you may go."

EXPLANATION OF
Words & Idioms

Angelus: (n) a church bell that rings to call Catholics to prayer; it is rung morning afternoon and evening in remembrance of the Annunciation (the announcement that Mary would give birth to Christ).

Ba, be bi, bo, bu: a chant that children use to learn their vowels and consonants.

Bear: (v) to put force upon.

Bustle: (n) excited and noisy movement.

Draft: (n) a requirement that all males must go into the armed forces without choice.

Fancy! (interj) Imagine that!

Fish-hook: (n) probably a reference to the writing practice of drawing fish-hook loops prior to learning to write.

Frilled: (adj) having decorative ruffles around the sleeve or neck.

Hopvine: (n) a plant that has a long and slender stalk, similar to ivy, that climbs up and around surfaces. It produces a fruit, hops, that is used in beer.

Logical: (adj) something that makes the most sense; has the least amount of confusion.

Primer: (n) an elementary school textbook that teaches children to read.

Prussia: (n) a former European kingdom that included northern Germany and Poland but fell and became independent countries after World War II.

Saar: (n) a river in northeastern France

Spectacles: (n) eye glasses.

Twine: (v) to wrap around.

Vive La France! (French) basically means "long live France!" A term used in open defiance of a foreign power.

Study Questions

1. What did you learn from this last lesson?

2. Does this last lesson apply to us in our modern day as well? Explain your answer.

3. Why does the narrator pity M. Hamel?

4. By about 1900 most of the French in Alsace, the location of this story, could understand German, but would not speak it at home or the in the streets. Korea suffered a similar fate under Japanese rule. Does this make you appreciate your own language even more now that you have read the story? Explain your answer.

5. "Then, from one thing to another, M. Hamel went on to talk of the French language, saying that it was the most beautiful language in the world - the clearest, the most logical; that we must guard it among us and never forget it, because when a people are enslaved, as long as they hold on to their language it is as if they had the key to their prison." What does the author mean by this sentence? How is language the key to breaking free from enslavement?

6. What war is Alphonse referring to? What was the eventual outcome of France in that war?

7. How can this story be applied to any subject that we study? What is the moral of this story in regards to this? Explain your answer.

8. What does this story say about the profession of a teacher? What is your opinion of this? How valuable is a teacher to the survival of a nation's identity? Explain your answer.

X. THE WIVES OF THE DEAD

by Nathaniel Hawthorne

INTRODUCTION OF THE AUTHOR:
Nathaniel Hawthorne (1804-1864)

Considered one of America's most important writers as well as the most modern, Nathaniel Hawthorne was born in Salem, Massachusetts, on July 4, 1844. His father was a ship captain that had died at sea when he was four years old. After his father's death, his family moved in with his mother's parents in a country estate where he read eagerly and fell in love with the countryside. He returned to Salem in 1821 to attend Bowdoin College where he met the three most important and influential friends in his life: Horatio Bridge, a later United States Navel officer, who helped Hawthorne publish his first book, *Fanshawe* (1828), published under the pseudonym Peter Parley; Henry Wadsworth Longfellow, the later famed poet of *Hiawatha*, who reviewed Hawthorne's first book; and Franklin Pierce, who would later become the 14th President of the United States and helped Hawthorne be appointed the Consul to Liverpool in 1853.

After graduation, Hawthorne turned to writing, a profession that wasn't looked upon very well since most books were brought over from England and most short story authors used pseudonyms to hide the fact that they actually worked in a low paying industry. His first novel *Fanshawe* (1828), drew upon his college experiences and was published using his own money. He then spent twelve lonely years writing and trying to make a name for himself in an industry that just didn't care. Then in 1837,

Hawthorne published *Twice-Told Tales*, a collection of his short stories that finally earned him his sought after recognition. Just to make money to support his writing lifestyle, however, Hawthorne started work at the Boston Custom House in 1839 that later led to his employment at the Salem Custom House in 1846 that is introduced in his most popular work, *The Scarlet Letter* (1850). By 1842, Hawthorne had earned enough money to marry Sophia Peabody, who was of similar temperament and loved his works of fiction. Though he later lost his job at the Salem Custom House when the country changed Presidents, he wrote a favorable campaign biography for his old friend Pierce, who was later elected President in 1852. As a reward for his help, Pierce appointed him Consul to Liverpool, which improved his financial situation considerably.

Hawthorne wrote his most famous novels after 1850, which started with a lasting friendship with author Herman Melville of *Moby Dick* (1851) fame. Melville was a fan of Hawthorne's writing, especially his short story collection *Mosses from an Old Manse* (1846). He went on to write *The Scarlet Letter* (1850), *The House of the Seven Gables* (1851), *The Blithedale Romance* (1852), and *The Marble Faun* (1860), which was written while he lived in Italy, all recognized as great modern romances. Hawthorne returned the favor through inspiring Melville to write his grand novel *Moby Dick* which he dedicated by writing, "In Token of my admiration for his genius, This book is inscibed to Nathaniel Hawthorne."

By 1860, Hawthorne's health was deteriorating that only

excellorated with stress of the coming Civil War (1861-1865). Nathaniel Hawthorne died on May 18, 1864, after traveling through the White Mountains, New Hampshire, with ex-president Piece.

Synopsis

Margaret and Mary, two newlywed brides of brothers, sit in front of the cooling embers of a fireplace mourning the recent deaths of their husbands, one a landsman, the other a sailor. The first had been killed by a war in Canada (most probably the War of 1812), the other when his ship sank during a storm. Friends and well wishers have come to pay their respects for the recently deceased and widows, yet the women find no comfort in their words. Both retire to their bedrooms where they face their grief alone. Mary eventually falls into a light sleep, while Margaret rolls around in bed, unable to find any comfort as she sees the phantom memories of her past, happy life. During her lowest point of grieving, a knock comes to the door. The joy of hearing news of her husband's return are now long gone, she refuses to answer the door. Yet there is always hope that good news could come from the late caller.

Margaret answers the door and the innkeeper steps into the light. He has recently received information that her husband is in fact alive and well and on his way with thirteen other survivors of the war on the next train. Such joy overwhelms Margaret that she runs to her sister-in-law's room to tell her the good news; but how can she? With Mary's husband missing at sea, it doesn't seem right to burden her with such selfish good news. She decides to let Mary sleep in peace. Margaret decides to retire to bed, and with the comfort of her husband returning, she drifts into a deep slumber.

Later in the night, Mary wakes from a dream in time to hear knocking at the door. Realization of her sorrow soon settles in, but fearing the knocking will wake Margaret, she rushes to answer the door. A young sailor, Mary's ex-lover, is standing at the door. His good news outweighs his presence at her door as he tells her he saw her husband returning from sea. He and three others had survived the sinking of their ship by floating on a log, and he should return by morning. Joy overwhelms Mary as well as she turns to tell her good news to Margaret. Entering her sister-in-law's room she is about to wake her, when she notes the deep sleep that has overcome Margaret and the smile on her lips. Mistaking it as a pleasant dream, Mary remembers that such glad tidings can only act as a further torment for Margaret who still mourns the death of her husband and waking her from such a pleasant dream could only be thought of as cruel. Adjusting the covers over her sleeping sister, thoughts of her joy and Margaret's suffering overwhelm Mary. A tear drops on Margaret's cheek only to awaken her...

TEXT

The following story, the simple and domestic incidents of which may be deemed scarcely worth relating, after such a lapse of time, awakened some degree of interest, a hundred years ago, in a principal seaport of the Bay Province. The rainy twilight of an autumn day; a parlor on the second floor of a small house, plainly furnished, as beseemed the middling circumstances of its inhabitants, yet decorated with little curiosities from beyond the sea, and a few delicate specimens of Indian manufacture, □ these are the only particulars to be premised in regard to scene and season. Two young and comely women sat together by the fireside, nursing their mutual and peculiar sorrows. They were the recent brides of two brothers, a sailor and a landsman, and two successive days had brought tidings of the death of each, by the chances of Canadian warfare, and the tempestuous Atlantic. The universal sympathy excited by this bereavement, drew numerous condoling guests to the habitation of the widowed sisters. Several, among whom was the minister, had remained till the verge of evening; when one by one, whispering many comfortable passages of Scripture, that were answered by more abundant tears, they took their leave and departed to their own happier homes. The mourners, though not insensible to the kindness of their friends, had yearned to be left alone. United, as they had been, by the relationship of the living, and now more closely so by that of the dead, each felt as if whatever consolation her grief admitted, were to be found in the bosom of the other. They joined their hearts, and wept together silently. But after an hour of such indulgence, one of the sisters, all of whose emotions were influenced by her mild, quiet, yet not feeble character, began to recollect the precepts of resignation and endurance, which piety had taught her, when she did not think to need them. Her misfortune, besides, as earliest known, should earliest cease to interfere with her regular course of duties; accordingly, having placed the table before the fire, and arranged a frugal meal, she took the hand of her companion.

"Come, dearest sister; you have eaten not a morsel to-day," she said. "Arise, I pray you, and let us ask a blessing on that which is provided for us."

Her sister-in-law was of a lively and irritable temperament, and the first pangs of her sorrow had been expressed by shrieks and passionate lamentation. She now shrunk from Mary's words, like a wounded sufferer from a hand that revives the throb.

"There is no blessing left for me, neither will I ask it," cried Margaret, with a fresh burst of tears. "Would it were His will that I might never taste food more."

Yet she trembled at these rebellious expressions, almost as soon as they were uttered, and, by degrees, Mary succeeded in bringing her sister's mind nearer to the situation of her own. Time went on, and their usual hour of repose arrived. The brothers and their brides, entering the married state with no more than the slender means which then sanctioned such a step, had confederated themselves in one household, with equal rights to the parlor, and claiming exclusive privileges in two sleeping rooms contiguous to it. Thither the widowed ones retired, after heaping ashes upon the dying embers of their fire, and placing a lighted lamp upon the hearth. The doors of both chambers were left open, so that a part of the interior of each, and the beds with their unclosed curtains, were reciprocally visible. Sleep did not steal upon the sisters at one and the same time. Mary experienced the effect often consequent upon grief quietly borne, and soon sunk into temporary forgetfulness, while Margaret became more disturbed and feverish, in proportion as the night advanced with its deepest and stillest hours. She lay listening to the drops of rain, that came down in monotonous succession, unswayed by a breath of wind; and a nervous impulse continually caused her to lift her head from the pillow, and gaze into Mary's chamber and the intermediate apartment. The cold light of the lamp threw the shadows of the furniture up against the wall, stamping them immoveably there, except when they were shaken by a sudden flicker of the flame. Two vacant arm-chairs were in their old positions on opposite sides of the hearth, where the brothers had been wont to sit in young and laughing dignity, as heads of families; two humbler seats were near them, the true thrones of that little empire, where Mary and herself had exercised in love, a power that love had won. The cheerful radiance of the fire had shone upon the happy circle, and the dead glimmer of the lamp might have befitted their reunion now. While Margaret groaned in bitterness, she heard a knock at the street-door.

"How would my heart have leapt at that sound but yesterday!" thought she, remembering the anxiety with which she had long awaited tidings from her husband. "I care not for it now; let them begone, for I will not arise."

But even while a sort of childish fretfulness made her thus resolve, she was breathing hurriedly, and straining her ears to catch a repetition of the summons. It is difficult to be convinced of the death of one whom we have deemed another self. The knocking was now renewed in slow and regular strokes, apparently given with the soft end of a doubled fist, and was accompanied by words, faintly heard through several thicknesses of wall. Margaret looked to her sister's chamber, and beheld her still lying in the depths of sleep. She arose, placed her foot upon the floor, and slightly arrayed herself, trembling between fear and eagerness as she did so.

"Heaven help me!" sighed she. "I have nothing left to fear, and methinks I am ten times more a coward than ever."

Seizing the lamp from the hearth, she hastened to the window that overlooked the street-door. It was a lattice, turning upon hinges; and having thrown it back, she stretched her head a little way into the moist atmosphere. A lantern was reddening the front of the house, and melting its light in the neighboring puddles, while a deluge of darkness overwhelmed every other object. As the window grated on its hinges, a man in a broad brimmed hat and blanket-coat, stepped from under the shelter of the projecting story, and looked upward to discover whom his application had aroused. Margaret knew him as a friendly innkeeper of the town.

"What would you have, Goodman Parker?" cried the widow.

"Lack-a-day, is it you, Mistress Margaret?" replied the innkeeper. "I was afraid it might be your sister Mary; for I hate to see a young woman in trouble, when I haven't a word of comfort to whisper her."

"For Heaven's sake, what news do you bring?" screamed Margaret.

"Why, there has been an express through the town within this half hour," said Goodman Parker, "travelling from the eastern jurisdiction with letters from the governor and council. He tarried at my house to refresh himself with a drop and a morsel, and I asked him what tidings on the frontiers. He tells me we had the better in the skirmish you wot of, and that thirteen men reported slain are well and sound, and your husband among them. Besides, he is appointed of the escort to bring the captivated Frenchers and Indians home to the province jail. I judged you wouldn't mind being broke of your rest, and so I stept over to tell you. Good night."

So saying, the honest man departed; and his lantern gleamed along the street, bringing to view indistinct shapes of things, and the fragments of a world, like order glimmering through chaos, or memory roaming over the past. But Margaret staid not to watch these picturesque effects. Joy flashed into her heart, and lighted it up at once, and breathless, and with winged steps, she flew to the bedside of her sister. She paused, however, at the door of the chamber, while a thought of pain broke in upon her.

"Poor Mary!" said she to herself. "Shall I waken her, to

feel her sorrow sharpened by my happiness? No; I will keep it within my own bosom till the morrow."

She approached the bed to discover if Mary's sleep were peaceful. Her face was turned partly inward to the pillow, and had been hidden there to weep; but a look of motionless contentment was now visible upon it, as if her heart, like a deep lake, had grown calm because its dead had sunk down so far within. Happy is it, and strange, that the lighter sorrows are those from which dreams are chiefly fabricated. Margaret shrunk from disturbing her sister-in-law, and felt as if her own better fortune, had rendered her involuntarily unfaithful, and as if altered and diminished affection must be the consequence of the disclosure she had to make. With a sudden step, she turned away. But joy could not long be repressed, even by circumstances that would have excited heavy grief at an other moment. Her mind was thronged with delightful thoughts, till sleep stole on and transformed them to visions, more delightful and more wild, like the breath of winter, (but what a cold comparison!) working fantastic tracery upon a window.

When the night was far advanced, Mary awoke with a sudden start. A vivid dream had latterly involved her in its unreal life, of which, however, she could only remember that it had been broken in upon at the most interesting point. For a little time, slumber hung about her like a morning mist, hindering her from perceiving the distinct outline of her situation. She listened with imperfect consciousness to two or three volleys of a rapid and eager knocking; and first she deemed the noise a matter of course, like the breath she drew; next, it appeared a thing in which she had no concern; and lastly, she became aware that it was a summons necessary to be obeyed. At the same moment, the pang of recollection darted into her mind; the pall of sleep was thrown back from the face of grief; the dim light of the chamber, and the objects therein revealed, had retained all her suspended ideas, and restored them as soon as she unclosed her eyes. Again, there was a quick peal upon the street-door. Fearing that her sister would also be disturbed, Mary wrapped herself in a cloak and hood, took the lamp from the hearth, and hastened to the window. By some accident, it had been left unhasped, and yielded easily to her hand.

"Who's there?" asked Mary, trembling as she looked forth.

The storm was over, and the moon was up; it shone upon broken clouds above, and below upon houses black with moisture, and upon little lakes of the fallen rain, curling into silver beneath the quick enchantment of a breeze. A young man in a sailor's dress, wet as if he had come out of the depths of the sea, stood alone under the window. Mary recognized him as one whose livelihood was gained by short voyages along the coast; nor did she forget, that, previous to her marriage, he had been an unsuccessful wooer of her own.

"What do you seek here, Stephen?" said she.

"Cheer up, Mary, for I seek to comfort you," answered the rejected lover. "You must know I got home not ten minutes ago, and the first thing my good mother told me was the news about your husband. So, without saying a word to the old woman, I clapt on my hat, and ran out of the house. I couldn't have slept a wink before speaking to you, Mary, for the sake of old times."

"Stephen, I thought better of you!" exclaimed the widow, with gushing tears, and preparing to close the lattice; for she was no whit inclined to imitate the first wife of Zadig.

"But stop, and hear my story out," cried the young sailor. "I tell you we spoke a brig yesterday afternoon, bound in from Old England. And who do you think I saw standing on deck, well and hearty, only a bit thinner than he was five months ago?"

Mary leaned from the window, but could not speak.

"Why, it was your husband himself," continued the generous seaman. "He and three others saved themselves on a spar when the Blessing turned bottom upwards. The brig will beat into the bay by daylight, with this wind, and you'll see him here tomorrow. There's the comfort I bring you, Mary, and so good night."

He hurried away, while Mary watched him with a doubt of waking reality, that seemed stronger or weaker as he alternately entered the shade of the houses, or emerged into the broad streaks of moonlight. Gradually, however, a blessed flood of conviction swelled into her heart, in strength enough to overwhelm her, had its increase been more abrupt. Her first impulse was to rouse her sister-in-law, and communicate the new-born gladness. She opened the chamber-door, which had been closed in the course of the night, though not latched, advanced to the bedside, and was about to lay her hand upon the slumberer's shoulder. But then she remembered that

Margaret would awake to thoughts of death and woe, rendered not the less bitter by their contrast with her own felicity. She suffered the rays of the lamp to fall upon the unconscious form of the bereaved one. Margaret lay in unquiet sleep, and the drapery was displaced around her; her young check was rosy-tinted, and her lips half opened in a vivid smile; an expression of joy, debarred its passage by her sealed eyelids, struggled forth like incense from the whole countenance.

"My poor sister! you will waken too soon from that happy dream," thought Mary.

Before retiring, she set down the lamp and endeavored to arrange the bed-clothes, so that the chill air might not do harm to the feverish slumberer. But her hand trembled against Margaret's neck, a tear also fell upon her cheek, and she suddenly awoke.

EXPLANATION OF Words & Idioms

Application: (n) a diligent effort.

Bay Province: (n) a province of the Massachusetts Bay.

Beseem: (v) to suit.

Brig: (n) a sailing ship with two masts (the pole that holds the sails).

Clap: (v) to put on quickly and firmly.

Comely: (adj) attractive.

Confederate: (v) to join together.

Deluge: (n) an overwhelming amount; a flood.

Felicity: (n) luck (no longer used).

First wife of Zadig: *Zadig* is a famous novel by French philosopher Voltaire, where Zadig's wife, Azora, was a woman who misunderstood a widow's slip from faithfulness toward her dead husband, only to make the same mistake herself.

Fretfulness: (n) fear.

Goodman: (n) a term no longer used for a married man or male head of the household.

Lack-a-day: (interj) a term no longer used to express regret or disapproval.

Landsman: (n) a person who lives and works on land.

Lattice: (n) A window with strips of wood overlapped in a crisscross pattern.

Morsel: (n) a small bit of food; a crumb.

Pall: (n) a murky or oppressing feeling

Parlor: (n) a room in a house where people can sit and relax.

Peal: (v) a loud burst of noise.

Reciprocally: (adj) both.

Resignation: (n) acceptance of something that is unavoidable.

Specimen: (n) a sample.

Thronged: (adj) crowded.

Unhasped: (adj) unhooked; unlocked.

Whit: (n) a little bit.

Wooer: (n) a man who tries to gain the love of a woman.

Study Questions

1. Hawthorne is very gifted in creating a sense of place in his fiction. He writes with very vivid details to create a world the reader can actual enter and feel. What specific role does the setting play in the story as a whole?

2. What details in the story help establish the mood? How do they make you feel about the house? What does the house actually feel like?

3. Weather plays an important role of setting the mood of the story as well. How does Hawthorne use weather to symbolize the change in the story? How does he use weather to symbolize the change in Mary and Margaret?

4. Reread the story. This time read carefully the revelation that the sisters' husbands are still alive. Is there a possibility that these women had dreamed their good fortune? Use the text to support your answer.

5. Both sisters refuse to awaken the other with their good news. Are there any clues in the story that either of the sisters would have been jealous of such good news? Would either of the sisters have tried to make the other suffer as she still does? Support your answer with words from the text.

6. Why does Hawthorne end his story with Mary accidentally waking Margaret up? What is the purpose of this kind of ending? Do you think Margaret knew and was faking being asleep? What do you think happens next? Write an ending to the story.

7. What would you say the main message of this story is?

XI. A CHILD'S CHRISTMAS IN WALES

by Dylan Thomas

INTRODUCTION OF THE AUTHOR:

Dylan Thomas (1914-1953)

Born on October 27, 1914 in the seaport town of Swansea, Wales, Dylan Marlais Thomas received his education at the Samsea Grammar School where his father was the senior English master. Having a Welsh heritage while brought up on English language helped Thomas understand the rhythms of Welsh that he adapted into his English poetry, which he started to write while he was still in school. He wrote poems at an early age and published them for his school paper. He later gave up his option to attend university, much to his father's distress, and started work as a newspaper reporter for the *South Wales Evening Post*. Though he had written poems before, it was not until he won a poetry contest held by a popular newspaper in 1933 that people started to take notice. He decided to publish a book of poems the following year, *Eighteen Poems*, which established him as a promising young poet uprooting lost romantic ideals. In 1936, he published another set of poems, *Twenty Five Poems* that confirmed him as a poet who could continue to produce great poetry.

With his career set, Thomas moved to London where he continued to write, this time trying his hand at prose, successfully, and as a lecturer. He published an autobiographical book called *Portrait of the Artist as a Young Dog* (1940), which showed his wit by his paying homage to James Joyce, as well as a dramatic understanding of his life and surroundings. Perhaps one of his best remembered short stories is "A Child's Christmas in Wales" (1955) that conjured up fond memories of his childhood in Swansea. He also started work as a broadcaster, where his rhetorical style of speaking was perfect for the radio. During World War II he worked for the BBC, using his voice and fame to bring some sanity back from the chaos of the German bombardment of London.

Thomas suffered from a mental breakdown that sent him back to Wales, and then sudden financial difficulties started him on his first American poetry reading tour in January of 1950. His Bohemian lifestyle became legendary as he read his poetry with theatrical fervor, got into public disputes that often angered and shocked Academics, and drank heavily. With the success of his tour, he arranged several more in 1952 and 53. 1953, proved to be a year to remember. He took the opportunity to read one of his greatest poems, *Under Milk Wood* (1954), that became even more memorable, for it was his last. Due to his rowdy lifestyle and exuberant drinking bouts, Thomas suffered from alcoholism. After one long drinking binge in New York and his famous poetry readings, Thomas died at the young age of 39.

Synopsis

This is actually Dylan Thomas' recollection of many Christmases past rather than a narrative tale. It can be read as an older man thinking back upon the mystery and wonder of Christmas as seen through the eyes of a child and how such a memory can be experienced again in the present. It starts with Thomas thinking back to his youth in a coastal town, perhaps Swansea in Wales, Great Britain. It is not so much a memory of one Christmas Eve but of his best memory of every Christmas Eve as a child. He remembers the abundant snowfall and the snowball fights that ensued. He remembers one Christmas Eve he was with his friend, Jim, throwing snowballs at cats, pretending the cats were wild beasts and they were Eskimos. Jim's house catches on fire and they rush into the house with their arms full of snowballs to throw on the fire. He remembers there being no fire but a lot of smoke. The firemen come and hose down the living room.

Even as Thomas remembers back, the voice of a child interjects into his thoughts as he describes the snow being different then than now, as if it grew out of the ground and trees and saturated the landscape like a fairy land. He talks of the postmen of yesteryear as being nostalgic and fairy bells that rang from within, for they were the ones who brought the presents to their door, while the church bells clamored through the town. The presents were of all kinds and assortments, both useful and useless, but all were magical none-the-less.

The child within asks of Uncles and is answered that no Christmas is complete without the Uncles hanging around the parlors smoking and talking while he blew balloons too large that they burst and disturbed the distinguished gentlemen. He speaks of a day of caroling up the street until they come to a foreboding haunted house. All the boys, never wishing to show cowardice, stand before the door, singing carols until they hear a thin, ghostly voice singing with them from behind the door. Thinking it the voice of a ghost the boys turn tail and run to their houses.

Young Thomas would return to his house where his family is gathered to sing Christmas songs before he goes to bed. He retires to his room and looks out over the snow covered streets and the burning lights inside the houses with a sense of reverence and awe. Then he goes to sleep.

TEXT

One Christmas was so much like another, in those years around the sea-town corner now, out of all sound except the distant speaking of the voices I sometimes hear a moment before sleep, that I can never remember whether it snowed for six days and six nights when I was twelve or whether it snowed for twelve days and twelve nights when I was six. All the Christmases roll down toward the two-tongued sea, like a cold and headlong moon bundling down the sky that was our street; and they stop at the rim of the ice-edged fish-freezing waves, and I plunge my hands in the snow and bring out whatever I can find. In goes my hand into that wool-white bell-tongued ball of holidays resting at the rim of the carol-singing sea, and out come Mrs. Prothero and the firemen.

It was on the afternoon of the day of Christmas Eve, and I was in Mrs. Prothero's garden, waiting for cats, with her son Jim. It was snowing. It was always snowing at Christmas. December, in my memory, is white as Lapland, although there were no reindeers. But there were cats. Patient, cold and callous, our hands wrapped in socks, we waited to snowball the cats. Sleek and long as jaguars and horrible-whiskered, spitting and snarling, they would slide and sidle over the white back-garden walls, and the lynx-eyed hunters, Jim and I, fur-capped and moccasined trappers from Hudson Bay, off Mumbles Road, would hurl our deadly snowballs at the green of their eyes. The wise cats never appeared. We were so still, Eskimo-footed arctic marksmen in the muffling silence of the eternal snows - eternal, ever since Wednesday □ that we never heard Mrs. Prothero's first cry from her igloo at the bottom of the garden. Or, if we heard it at all, it was, to us, like the far-off challenge of our enemy and prey, the neighbor's polar cat. But soon the voice grew louder.

"Fire!" cried Mrs. Prothero, and she beat the dinner-gong.

And we ran down the garden, with the snowballs in our arms, toward the house; and smoke, indeed, was pouring out of the dining-room, and the gong was bombilating, and Mrs. Prothero was announcing ruin like a town crier in Pompeii. This was better than all the cats in Wales standing on the wall in a row. We bounded into the house, laden with snowballs, and stopped at the open door of the smoke-filled room. Something was burning all right; perhaps it was Mr. Prothero, who always slept there after midday dinner with a newspaper over his face. But he was standing in the middle of the room, saying, "A fine Christmas!" and smacking at the smoke with a slipper.

"Call the fire brigade," cried Mrs. Prothero as she beat the gong.

"They won't be here," said Mr. Prothero, "it's Christmas."

There was no fire to be seen, only clouds of smoke and Mr. Prothero standing in the middle of them, waving his slipper as though he were conducting.

"Do something," he said.

And we threw all our snowballs into the smoke □ I think we missed Mr. Prothero □ and ran out of the house to the telephone box.

"Let's call the police as well," Jim said.

"And the ambulance."

"And Ernie Jenkins, he likes fires."

But we only called the fire brigade, and soon the fire engine came and three tall men in helmets brought a hose into the house and Mr. Prothero got out just in time before they turned it on. Nobody could have had a noisier Christmas Eve. And when the firemen turned off the hose and were standing in the wet, smoky room, Jim's Aunt, Miss Prothero, came downstairs and peered in at them. Jim and I waited, very quietly, to hear what she would say to them. She said the right thing, always. She looked at the three tall firemen in their shining helmets, standing among the smoke and cinders and dissolving snowballs, and she said, "Would you like anything to read?"

Years and years ago, when I was a boy, when there were wolves in Wales, and birds the color of red-flannel petticoats whisked past the harp-shaped hills, when we sang and wallowed all night and day in caves that smelt like Sunday afternoons in damp front farmhouse parlors, and we chased, with the jawbones of deacons, the English and the bears, before the motor car, before the wheel, before the duchess-faced horse, when we rode the daft and happy hills bareback, it snowed and it snowed. But here a small boy says: "It snowed last year, too. I made a snowman and my brother knocked it down and I knocked my brother down and then we had tea."

"But that was not the same snow," I say. "Our snow was not only shaken from white wash buckets down the sky, it came shawling out of the ground and swam and drifted out of the arms and hands and bodies of the trees; snow grew overnight on the roofs of the houses like a pure and grandfather moss, minutely-ivied the walls and settled on the postman, opening the gate, like a dumb, numb thunder-storm of white, torn Christmas cards."

"Were there postmen then, too?"

"With sprinkling eyes and wind-cherried noses, on spread, frozen feet they crunched up to the doors and mittened on them manfully. But all that the children could hear was a ringing of bells."

"You mean that the postman went rat-a-tat-tat and the doors rang?"

"I mean that the bells the children could hear were inside them."

"I only hear thunder sometimes, never bells."

"There were church bells, too."

"Inside them?"

"No, no, no, in the bat-black, snow-white belfries, tugged by bishops and storks. And they rang their tidings over the bandaged town, over the frozen foam of the powder and ice-cream hills, over the crackling sea. It seemed that all the churches boomed for joy under my window; and the weathercocks crew for Christmas, on our fence."

"Get back to the postmen."

"They were just ordinary postmen, fond of walking and dogs and Christmas and the snow. They knocked on the doors with blue knuckles ...."

"Ours has got a black knocker...."

"And then they stood on the white Welcome mat in the little, drifted porches and huffed and puffed, making ghosts with their breath, and jogged from foot to foot like small boys wanting to go out."

"And then the presents?"

"And then the Presents, after the Christmas box. And the cold postman, with a rose on his button-nose, tingled down the tea-tray-slithered run of the chilly glinting hill. He went in his ice-bound boots like a man on fishmonger' s slabs. He wagged his bag like a frozen camel's hump, dizzily turned the corner on one foot, and, by God, he was gone."

"Get back to the Presents."

"There were the Useful Presents: engulfing mufflers of the old coach days, and mittens made for giant sloths; zebra scarfs of a substance like silky gum that could be tug-o'-warred down to the galoshes; blinding tam-o'-shanters like patchwork tea cozies and bunny-suited busbies and balaclavas for victims of head-shrinking tribes; from aunts who always wore wool next to the skin there were mustached and rasping vests that made you wonder why the aunts had any skin left at all; and once I had a little crocheted nose bag from an aunt now, alas, no longer whinnying with us. And pictureless books in which small boys, though warned with quotations not to, would skate on Farmer Giles' pond and did and drowned; and books that told me everything about the wasp, except why."

"Go on the Useless Presents."

"Bags of moist and many-colored jelly babies and a folded flag and a false nose and a tram-conductor's cap and a machine that punched tickets and rang a bell; never a catapult; once, by mistake that no one could explain, a little hatchet; and a celluloid duck that made, when you pressed it, a most unducklike sound, a mewing moo that an ambitious cat might make who wished to be a cow; and a painting book in which I could make the grass, the trees, the sea and the animals any colour I pleased, and still the dazzling sky-blue sheep are grazing in the red field under the rainbow-billed and pea-green birds. Hardboileds, toffee, fudge and allsorts, crunches, cracknels, humbugs, glaciers, marzipan, and butterwelsh for the Welsh. And troops of bright tin soldiers who, if they could not fight, could always run. And Snakes-and-Families and Happy Ladders. And Easy Hobbi-Games for Little Engineers, complete with instructions. Oh, easy for Leonardo! And a whistle to make the dogs bark to wake up the old man next door to make him beat on the wall with his stick to shake our picture off the wall. And a packet of cigarettes: you put one in your mouth and you stood at the corner of the street and you waited for hours, in vain, for an old lady to scold you for smoking a cigarette, and then with a smirk you ate it. And then it was breakfast under the balloons."

"Were there Uncles like in our house?"

"There are always Uncles at Christmas. The same Uncles. And on Christmas mornings, with dog-disturbing whistle and sugar fags, I would scour the swatched town for the news of the little world, and find always a dead bird by the Post Office or the white deserted swings; perhaps a robin, all but one of his fires out. Men and women wading or scooping back from chapel, with taproom noses and wind-bussed cheeks, all albinos, huddles their stiff black jarring feathers against the irreligious snow. Mistletoe hung from the gas brackets in all the front parlors; there was sherry and walnuts and bottled beer and crackers by the dessertspoons; and cats in their fur-abouts watched the fires; and the high-heaped fire spat, all ready for the chestnuts and the mulling pokers. Some few large men sat in the front parlors, without their collars, Uncles almost certainly, trying their new cigars, holding them out judiciously at arms' length, returning them to their mouths, coughing, then holding them out again as though waiting for the explosion; and some few small aunts, not wanted in the kitchen, nor anywhere else for that matter, sat on the very edges of their chairs, poised and brittle, afraid to break, like faded cups and saucers."

Not many those mornings trod the piling streets: an old man always, fawn-bowlered, yellow-gloved and, at this time of year, with spats of snow, would take his constitutional to the white bowling green and back, as he would take it wet or fire on Christmas Day or Doomsday; sometimes two hale young men, with big pipes blazing, no overcoats and wind blown scarfs, would trudge, unspeaking, down to the forlorn sea, to work up an appetite, to blow away the fumes, who knows, to walk into the waves until nothing of them was left but the two curling smoke clouds of their inextinguishable briars. Then I would be slap-dashing home, the gravy smell of the dinners of others, the bird smell, the brandy, the pudding and mince, coiling up to my nostrils, when out of a snow-clogged side lane would come a boy the spit of myself, with a pink-tipped cigarette and the violet past of a black eye, cocky as a bullfinch, leering all to himself. I hated him on sight and sound, and would be about to put my dog whistle to my lips and blow him off the face of Christmas when suddenly he, with a violet wink, put *his* whistle to *his* lips and blew so stridently, so high, so exquisitely loud, that gobbling faces, their cheeks bulged with goose, would press against their tinsled windows, the whole length of the white echoing street. For dinner we had turkey and blazing pudding, and after dinner the Uncles sat in front of the fire, loosened all buttons, put their large moist hands over their watch chains, groaned a little and slept. Mothers, aunts and sisters scuttled to and fro, bearing tureens. Auntie Bessie, who had already been frightened, twice, by a clock-work mouse, whimpered at the sideboard and had some elderberry wine. The dog was sick. Auntie Dosie had to have three aspirins, but Auntie Hannah, who liked port, stood in the middle of the snowbound back yard, singing like a big-bosomed thrush. I would blow up balloons to see how big they would blow up to; and then, when they burst, which they all did, the Uncles jumped and rumbled. In the rich and heavy afternoon, the Uncles breathing like dolphins and the snow descending, I would sit among festoons and Chinese lanterns and nibble dates and try to make a model man-o'-war, following the Instructions for Little Engineers, and produce what might be mistaken for a sea-going tramcar. Or I would go out, my bright new boots squeaking, into the white world, on to the seaward hill, to call on Jim and Dan and Jack and to pad through the still streets, leaving huge deep footprints on the hidden pavements.

"I bet people will think there's been hippos."

"What would you do if you saw a hippo coming down our street?"

"I'd go like this, bang! I'd throw him over the railings and roll him down the hill and then I'd tickle him under the ear and he'd wag his tail."

"What would you do if you saw two hippos?"

Iron-flanked and bellowing he-hippos clanked and battered through the scudding snow toward us as we passed Mr. Daniel's house.

"Let's post Mr. Daniel a snow-ball through his letter box."

"Let's write things in the snow."

"Let's write, 'Mr. Daniel looks like a spaniel' all over his lawn."

Or we walked on the white shore. "Can the fishes see it's snowing?"

The silent one-clouded heavens drifted on to the sea. Now we were snow-blind travelers lost on the north hills, and vast dewlapped dogs, with flasks round their necks, ambled and shambled up to us, baying "Excelsior." We returned home through the poor streets where only a few children fumbled with bare red fingers in the wheel-rutted snow and cat-called after us, their voices fading away, as we trudged uphill, into the cries of the dock birds and the hooting of ships out in the whirling bay. And then, at tea the recovered Uncles would be jolly; and the ice cake loomed in the center of the table like a marble grave. Auntie Hannah laced her tea with rum, because it was only once a year.

Bring out the tall tales now that we told by the fire as the gaslight bubbled like a diver. Ghosts whooed like owls in the long nights when I dared not look over my shoulder; animals lurked in the cubbyhole under the stairs where the gas meter ticked. And I remember that we went singing carols once, when there wasn't the shaving of a moon to light the flying streets. At the end of a long road was a drive that led to a large house, and we stumbled up the darkness of the drive that night, each one of us afraid, each one holding a stone in his hand in case, and all of us too brave to say a word. The wind through the trees made noises as of old and unpleasant and maybe webfooted men wheezing in caves. We reached the black bulk of the house.

"What shall we give them? Hark the Herald?"

"No," Jack said, "Good King Wencelas. I'll count three."

One, two three, and we began to sing, our voices high and seemingly distant in the snow-felted darkness round the house that was occupied by nobody we knew. We stood close together, near the dark door.

Good King Wencelas looked out

On the Feast of Stephen ...

And then a small, dry voice, like the voice of someone who has not spoken for a long time, joined our singing: a small, dry, eggshell voice from the other side of the door: a small dry voice through the keyhole. And when we stopped running we were outside our house; the front room was lovely; balloons floated under the hot-water-bottle-gulping gas; everything was good again and shone over the town.

"Perhaps it was a ghost," Jim said."

"Perhaps it was trolls," Dan said, who was always reading.

"Let's go in and see if there's any jelly left," Jack said. And we did that.

Always on Christmas night there was music. An uncle played the fiddle, a cousin sang "Cherry Ripe," and another uncle sang "Drake's Drum." It was very warm in the little house. Auntie Hannah, who had got on to the parsnip wine, sang a song about Bleeding Hearts and Death, and then another in which she said her heart was like a Bird's Nest; and then everybody laughed again; and then I went to bed. Looking through my bedroom window, out into the moonlight and the unending smoke-colored snow, I could see the lights in the windows of all the other houses on our hill and hear the music rising from them up the long, steadily falling night. I turned the gas down, I got into bed. I said some words to the close and holy darkness, and then I slept.

EXPLANATION OF
Words & Idioms

Balaclava: (n) a wool hood that covers the head and neck.

Bombilating: (v) humming.

Briar: (n) a smoking pipe.

Busby: (n) a formal fur hat.

Butterwelsh: (n) butterscotch candy. A humorous play with words since a Welshman isn't Scottish and wouldn't eat butterscotch.

Callous: (adj) without feeling.

Celluloid: (adj) artificial; not real.

Constitutional: (n) a regular walk taken for health.

Cracknel: (n) a hard crisp biscuit.

Daft: (adj) energetic and playful.

Deacon: (n) a cleric ranking below a priest.

Dewlapped: (adj) having a fold of loose skin hanging from the neck.

Excelsior: (n) perhaps a South African manufactured wine.

Fags: (slang) cigarettes.

Glaciers: (n) a white peppermint candy.

Hale: (adj) free from sickness; healthy.

Hudson Bay: (n) a large inland sea in Northern Canada.

Humbugs: (n) a stripped peppermint hard candy.

Jelly babies: (n) a British candy in the shape of babies.

Judiciously: (adv) sensibly or practically.

Lapland: (n) a region in Northern Europe mostly above the Arctic Circle.

Man-o'-war: (n) a sailing navy ship armed with cannons.

Marzipan: (n) an almond flavored candy.

Mince: (n) a pudding mixture of raisins, sugar, chopped apple, candied peel, spices etc.

Mull: (v) to heat and spice.

Pompeii: (n) a flourishing Roman colony in southern Italy. It was destroyed by a volcano in A.D. 79.

Port: (n) a sweet wine.

Shawl: (v) to cover as with a blanket.

Sidle: (v) to move sideways.

Slap-dash: (v) to go in a quick or careless manner.

Sloth: (n) a slow moving animal.

Stridently: (adj) loud.

Tam-o'-shanter: (n) a tight fitting Scottish hat.

Tureen: (n) a wide deep dish used for serving soups.

Wales: (n) a principality of the United Kingdom.

Wallow: (v) to enjoy or delight in.

Whinny: (v) the sound a horse makes.

Study Questions

1. Dylan Thomas is known mostly for his poetry. In what ways is this short story more poetic than dramatic?

2. Style is how the writer uses language to put his/her visions down in word format. Since Thomas is the actual narrator and not a fictional one, we see his hometown through his own eyes. How does this point of view form the story as a whole? What do we learn from his sense of humor, thinking, and behavior? Do you understand more about Thomas from this story than you do from his biography? Explain your answer.

3. What kind of language does Thomas use? Is it how ordinary people would speak, or is it an elevated style of speaking? What makes Thomas' vocabulary more elevated than the everyday speech? What effects does this type of writing have on the reader?

4. Would you say this story, or flashback, is like a fairytale? What makes it like a fairytale? Give examples from the story to support your answer.

5. Thomas is also well known for his poems and stories detailing the experiences of ordinary people. What are some examples of these experiences? How does the commonality of these experiences change with the elevated style of his language?

6. Thomas uses metaphors to breathe life into his narrative. Give some examples of his metaphors.

7. Look at some of the poetic metaphors that Thomas uses. What does he mean by "two-tongued sea," and what could "making ghosts with their breath" mean, and what is the meaning behind "the close and holy darkness"?

Glossary

Allegory
A literary work in which the characters and their situations clearly represent general qualities and types as, in an animal fable, ach animal may represent a type of human personality. Often the characters of allegory represent abstract vices or virtues such as avarice, charity, innocence, or prudery.

Ambiguity
Ambiguity refers to the fact that words can often have several meanings, thus making us uncertain what is meant.

Archetype
An archetype is a basic model from which copies are made. It can be argued that at the heart of all works of literature are certain simple patterns that embody fundamental human concerns, the primary concern being the place of people in the natural world.

Canon
Originally the term canon applied to the list of books in the Hebrew Bible and New Testament which was accepted by church authorities as genuine and having divine authority. Writings not admitted to the canon are called apocrypha. The Protestant and Catholic churches differ as to which writings are apocryphal.

Character
The people in a novel are referred to as characters. We

assess them on the basis of what the author tells us about them and on the basis of what they do and say. This is important: we must avoid loose conjecture about a character and establish everything from the evidence of the text. Another point to remember is that the characters are part of a broader pattern: they are members of a society, and the author's distinctive view of how people relate to society will be reflected in the presentation of every character. Details are not included just for their own sake but relate to the overall pattern of the novel.

Comic novels

Novels primarily intended to make us laugh. Students are sometimes grudging in their praise of comic novels, as they can appear lightweight compared to realistic novels, which present such a substantial picture of life. A common, but misguided approach is to ascribe some social purpose to the writer and then to argue that the comedy makes the social criticism entertaining.

Contradiction

Contradiction occurs where we are faced with two or ore meanings that cannot be reconciled or resolved. To this extent it overlaps with ambiguity, but there are important differences. Critics tend to use ambiguity to demonstrate the richness of the texts being discussed. Contradiction, however, which has become a central term in poststructuralist criticism, points to incoherences or divisions in a text that undermine its apparent stability.

Gothic novels

They concentrate on the more sensational side of romance; they depart from the social world, not to seek an ideal goal, but to explore the irrational passions of the mind.

Irony

Irony is a way of writing in which what is meant is contrary to what the words appear to say. Pope, for example, might praise someone extravagantly in his poetry, but the terms used can be so extravagant that they signal to the reader that the person referred to does not deserve such praise.

Metaphor

A figure of speech in which one thing is described in terms of another. A *simile* is very nearly the same, but, whereas metaphor identifies one thing with another, a simile involves the notion of similarity, using the words 'like' or 'as'.

Narrative structure

Narrative is the organization of a series of events into the form of a story. This is obviously what we have in novels; what is less obvious is how similar the narrative structure is in most novels.

Narrator

The narrator tells the story in a novel. Novels contain simple stories which, in their telling, become complicated. There are two overlapping ways by which the novelist can complicate matters. One is by introducing complications in the content: the inclusion of a mass of details about people, places and events makes the story seem substantial and real. The other way in which the writer can complicate matters is by the way in which he or she chooses to narrate the story: a story can be told in many ways, for every narrator will see things from a different point-of-view.

Paradox

A paradox is a statement that appears to be contradictory or inconsistent with common sense □ though it may be quite true.

Pathetic fallacy

It objects to the way in which poets attributed human feelings and actions to natural objects.

Plot

Plot is that framework of incidents, however simple or complex, upon which the narrative or drama is constructed, upon which the narrative or drama is constructed; the events of the depicted struggle, as organized into an artistic unit. The elements of plot are a beginning that presumes further action, a middle that presumes both previous and succeeding action, and an end that requires the preceding events but no succeeding action. The unity of the plot is thus the result of necessary relationship and order among the events, not that they center upon a single character.

Postmodernism
Like many of the 'post' terms of modern critical theory, postmodernism has a number of connected uses. In a literal sense it refers to those works of art that were written after the modernist period of the early twentieth century.

Realism
It is particularly associated with the nineteenth-century novel to refer to the idea that texts appear to represent 'the world' 'as it really is'. It means that they will select from their observations the material suitable for constructing a story that faithfully represents what they have understood. Realistic is the label we apply to those novels that seek to provide a convincing illusion of life as we normally think of it. Readers who are just beginning to study novels often feel most comfortable with realistic novels because they appear relatively straightforward. The realistic novel can seem like a clear window on the world □ and as readers we can become fully involved with the characters and events □ while non-realistic novels seem to look at the world through a distorting mirror, with the result that we are forced to consider the relationship between the work of art itself and life.

Romance
We use the term 'romance' to describe those novels where the story is more adventurous or more fanciful than in realistic novels. Something grander than the novel's familiar concern with social issues is involved, for 'romance' suggests a search for some truth beyond that

which we might encounter in ordinary experience. Both characters and events are removed from the everyday, so that there is always an air of the extraordinary about romance.

Satire
The humorous presentation of human folly or vice in such a way as to make it look ridiculous. The satirist aims to correct, by an exposure to ridicule, deviations from normal conduct or reasonable opinion. The chief tool of satire is to exaggerate deformities to the point at which their absurdity is unmistakably apparent.

Science fiction (Sci-Fi)
The informing impulse can be to present a world where the problems for ordinary life are transcended and where the characters can live a more heroic or more ordered life.

Stream of consciousness Technique
A technique which seeks to record the random flow of impressions through a character's mind.

Structure
The structure of a text is its overall shape and pattern. This is sometimes referred to as its form, though strictly speaking form is a more inclusive term which embraces every aspect of the work's technique.

Style
Style means the writer's characteristic manner of

expression. What in the end distinguishes one writer from another so that the experienced reader could identify a passage as coming from, say, a Lawrence novel is the style. Style change from age to age, but every novelist has his or her own 'voice'.

Utopian novel
They present a perfectly ordered society where all the problems of the real world have been eliminated. This is, however, more than simple day-dreaming: often the intention is that this should reflect back on the imperfections of the existing world.

INDEX

저자 약력

강옥선

부산대학교 박사학위 취득

동서대학교 영어학과 부교수

저서:

블레이크와 작은 천국(동인, 2004), 공저

Reading British Poetry(동인, 2004), 공저

논문: 낭만기 여성시인의 도덕적 감수성 읽기(2005)

블레이크의 예언시와 사회의식(2001)

스티븐 리더

캘리포니아 주립대학 석사학위 취득

동서대학교 전임강사(ISP 프로그램)

저서:

Reading British Poetry(동인, 2004), 공저

논문: Dracula as a Tragic Hero: The Illumination of Film on a Text(2006)